LAST TERM AT
MALORY TOWERS

LAST TERM AT
MALORY TOWERS

DEAN

First published in Great Britain 1951
Reissued 2004 by Dean
an imprint of Egmont UK Limited
239 Kensington High Street, London W8 6SA

ISBN 978 0 603 56167 2
3 5 7 9 10 8 6 4 2

Printed and bound in Singapore

Contents

1 First day

My last term! thought Darrell, as she got ready to go downstairs. My very last term! I shall be eighteen on my next birthday – I'm almost grown-up!

A yell came from below, 'Darrell! Aren't you *ever* coming? Daddy says do you mean to leave today or tomorrow?'

'Coming!' shouted back Darrell. She snatched up her tennis racket and her small suitcase and fled down the stairs, two at a time as usual.

Her young sister Felicity was there, waiting for her. Both were dressed in the orange and brown uniform of Malory Towers – dark brown coat and skirt, white blouse, orange tie, straw hat with orange band.

'It's the very last time I shall go off with you in the same uniform,' said Darrell, rather solemnly. 'Next term you'll be going alone, Felicity. How will you like it?'

'Not a bit,' said Felicity, quite cheerfully. 'Still, you'll be having a wonderful time yourself, going off to the University. Don't look so solemn.'

'Last times are always a bit horrid,' said Darrell. She went out to the car with Felicity. Their father was just about to begin a fanfare on the horn. Why, oh why was he always kept waiting like this? Didn't they *know* it was time to start?

'Thank goodness you've appeared at last,' he said. 'Get in. Now, where's your mother? Honestly, this family wants a daily shepherd to round up all its sheep! Ah, here she comes!'

As Mrs. Rivers got into the car, Felicity slipped out again. Her father didn't notice her, and started up the car. Darrell gave a shriek.

'Daddy, Daddy! Wait! Felicity's not in!'

He looked round in astonishment. 'But I saw her get in,' he said. 'Bless us all, where's she gone now?'

'She forgot to say good-bye to the kitten, I expect,' said Darrell, grinning. 'She has to say good-bye to everything, even the goldfish in the pond. I used to do that too – but I never wept over them all like Felicity!'

Felicity appeared again at top speed. She flung herself into the car, panting. 'Forgot to say good-bye to the gardener,' she said. 'He promised to look after my seedlings for me, and count how many strawberries come on my strawberry plants. Oh dear – it's so horrid to say good-bye to everything.'

'Well, don't then,' said Darrell.

'Oh, but I like to,' said Felicity. 'Once I've done a really *good* round of good-byes, I feel that I can look forward to school properly then. I say – I wonder if that awful Josephine is coming back! She kept saying something about going to America with those frightful people of hers, so I hope she has.'

'I hope she has too,' said Darrell, remembering the loud-voiced, bad-mannered Josephine Jones. 'She doesn't fit into Malory Towers somehow. I can't imagine why the Head took her.'

'Well – I suppose she thought Malory Towers might tone her down and make something of her,' said Felicity. 'It's not many people it doesn't alter for the better, really. Even me!'

'Gosh – has it done that?' said Darrell, pretending to

be surprised. 'I'm glad to know it. Oh dear – I wish it wasn't my last term. It seems no time at all since I was first setting out, six years ago, a little shrimp of twelve.'

'There you go again – coming over all mournful,' said Felicity, cheerfully. 'I can't think why you don't feel proud and happy – you've been games captain of one or two forms, you've been head-girl of forms – and now you're head-girl of the whole school, and have been for two terms! I shall never be that.'

'I hope you *will*,' said Darrell. 'Anyway, I'm glad Sally and I are leaving together and going to the same college. We shall still be with each other. Daddy, don't forget we're calling for Sally, will you?'

'I hadn't forgotten,' said her father. He took the road that led to Sally Hope's home. Soon they were swinging into the drive, and there, on the front steps, were Sally and her small sister of about six or seven.

'Hallo, Darrell, hallo, Felicity!' called Sally. 'I'm quite ready. Mother, where are you? Here are the Riverses.'

Sally's small sister called out loudly: 'I'm coming to Malory Towers one day – in six years' time.'

'Lucky you, Daffy!' called back Felicity. 'It's the best school in the world!'

Sally got in and squeezed herself between Felicity and Darrell. She waved good-bye and off they went again.

'It's the last time, Darrell!' she said. 'I wish it was the first!'

'Oh, don't *you* start now,' said Felicity. 'Darrell's been glooming all the journey, so far.'

'No cheek from you, Felicity Rivers!' said Sally, with a grin. 'You're only a silly little second-former, remember!'

3

'I'll be in the third form next term,' said Felicity. 'I'm creeping up the school! It takes a long time, though.'

'It seems a long time while it's happening,' said Sally. 'But now it's our last term, it all seems to have gone in a flash.'

They talked without stopping the whole of the journey, and then, as they drew near to Malory Towers, Sally and Darrell fell silent. They always loved the first glimpse of their lovely school, with its four great towers, one at each end.

They rounded a corner, and the eyes of all three fastened on a big square building of soft grey stone standing high up on a cliff that fell steeply down to the sea. At each end of the building stood rounded towers – North Tower, East, West and South. The school looked like an old castle. Beyond it was the dark-blue Cornish sea.

'We're nearly there!' sang Felicity. 'Daddy, go faster! Catch up the car in front. I'm sure Susan is in it.'

Just then a car roared by them, overtaking not only them but the one in front too. Mr. Rivers braked sharply as it passed him, almost forcing him into the hedge.

'That's Josephine's car!' called Felicity. 'Did you ever see such a monster?'

'Monster is just about the right word,' said her father, angrily. 'Forcing me into the side like that. What do they think they are doing, driving as fast as that in a country lane?'

'Oh, they always drive like that,' said Felicity. 'Jo's father can't bear driving under ninety miles an hour, he says. He's got four cars, Daddy, all as big as that.'

'He can keep them, then,' grunted her father, scarlet

with anger. He had just the same quick temper as Darrell's. 'I'll have a word with him about his driving if I see him at the school. A real road-hog!'

Felicity gave a squeal of delight. 'Oh, Daddy, you've hit on *just* the right name. He's exactly like a hog to look at – awfully fat, with little piggy eyes. Jo is just like him.'

'Then I hope she's no friend of yours,' said her father.

'She's not,' said Felicity. 'Susan's *my* friend. Here we are! Here's the gate. There's June! And Julie and Pam. Pam, PAM!'

'You'll deafen me,' said Mrs. Rivers, laughing. She turned to her husband. 'You won't be able to get near the steps up to the front door today, dear – there are too many cars, and the school coaches have brought up the train girls too.'

The big drive was certainly crowded. 'It's as noisy as a football crowd,' said Mr. Rivers with his sudden smile. 'It always amazes me that girls can make so much noise!'

Darrell, Felicity and Sally jumped out, clutching their rackets and bags. They were immediately engulfed in a crowd of excited girls.

'Darrell! You never wrote to me!'

'Felicity, have you seen Julie? She's been allowed to bring back her pony, Jack Horner! He's wizard!'

'Hallo, Sally! How tanned you are!'

'There's Alicia! Alicia, ALICIA! Betty! I say, everyone's arriving at once.'

A loud-voiced man, followed by a much overdressed woman, came pushing through the crowd, making his way to the enormous American car that had forced Mr. Rivers into the hedge.

'Well, good-bye, Jo,' he was saying. 'Mind you're bottom of the form. I always was! And don't you stand any nonsense from the mistresses, ha ha! You do what you like and have a good time.'

Darrell and Sally looked at one another in disgust. No wonder Jo was so awful if that was the way her father talked to her. And what a voice!

Jo Jones's father was obviously very pleased with himself indeed. He grinned round at the seething girls, threw out his chest, and clapped his fat little daughter on the back.

'Well, so long, Jo! And if you want any extra food, just let us know.'

He caught sight of Mr. Rivers looking at him, and he nodded and smiled. 'You got a girl here too?' he inquired, jovially.

'I have two,' said Mr. Rivers, in his clear confident voice. 'But let me tell you this, Mr. Jones – if I hadn't swung quickly into the hedge just now, when you cut in on that narrow lane, I might have had no daughters at all. Disgraceful driving!'

Mr. Jones was startled and taken aback. He glanced quickly round to see if anyone had heard. He saw that quite a lot of girls were listening and, after one look at Mr. Rivers's unsmiling face, he decided not to say a word more.

'Good for you, Daddy, good for you!' said Felicity, who was nearby. 'I bet nobody ever ticks him off – and now *you* have! Jo's just like him. Look, there she is.'

Jo scowled back at Felicity and Mr. Rivers. She hadn't heard what Felicity said about her, of course, but she had heard Felicity's father ticking off her own, and she didn't

6

like it a bit. Never mind – she would take it out of Felicity this term, if she could.

'We must go, darlings,' said Mrs. Rivers, leaning out of the car. 'Have you got everything? Good-bye, Darrell dear – and Felicity. Good-bye, Sally. Have a good term! The summer term is always the nicest of all!'

The car sped away. Felicity plunged into the milling crowd and was lost. Sally and Darrell went more sedately, as befitted two sixth-formers.

'It's nice to be at the top,' said Darrell. 'But I can't help envying those yelling, screaming lower-form kids. Just look at them. What a crowd!'

2 Arrivals old and new

Darrell and Sally went up the steps, and into the big hall. 'Let's go up to our study,' said Darrell. 'We can dump our things there and have a look round.'

They went up to the small, cosy room they shared between them. The sixth-formers were allowed to have these studies, one to every two girls, and both Sally and Darrell loved their small room.

They had put down a bright rug that Mrs. Rivers had given them, and each had a favourite picture on the walls. There were some old cushions provided by both mothers, and a few ornaments on the mantelpiece – mostly china or wooden horses and dogs.

'I wonder who'll have this room next term,' said Darrell, going to the window and looking out. 'It's one of the nicest.'

'*Quite* the nicest,' said Sally, sinking down into one of the small arm-chairs. 'I suppose one of the fifth-formers will have it. Lucky things!'

The sixth-formers had a common-room of their own, as well as studies. In the common-room was a radio, of course, a library, and various cupboards and shelves for the use of the girls. It looked out over the sea and was full of air and light and sun. The girls loved it.

'Better go down and report to Matron,' said Darrell, when they had unpacked their night-bags, and set out two clocks, three or four new ornaments, and Darrell had put a little table-cloth into a drawer, which she had brought back to use that term. It would look nice if they gave a tea-party, as they often did!

'Got your health certificate?' asked Sally. 'I wonder if Irene has got hers. She has remembered it faithfully for the last three or four terms. I'd love her to forget it just this last time.'

Darrell laughed. Irene's health certificate was a standing joke in the school. 'I've got Felicity's certificate with mine,' she said. 'I'd better give it to her. Come on, let's go down.'

They went down and found Matron, who was standing in the middle of a mob of girls. They were handing out health certificates to her and, in the case of the lower-formers, handing over their term's pocket-money too.

A voice greeted Darrell and Sally. 'Hallo! Here we are again!'

'Irene!' said Darrell and Sally at once. Irene grinned at them. She looked very little different from when Darrell had seen her the first time, six years back – older and taller, but still the same old untidy scatter-brain. But her looks belied her. Irene was a genius at music and brilliant at maths – it was only in ordinary things that she was a feather-head.

'Irene!' called Matron, who had been in despair over the girl's health certificate almost every term. 'Am I to isolate you this term, because you've forgotten your certificate again – or have you condescended to remember it?'

'Here you are, Matron!' said Irene, and handed an envelope to her. She winked at Darrell and Sally. Matron opened it. Out fell a photograph of Irene in a swimming-costume!

'Irene! This is a photograph!' said Matron, annoyed.

'Oh, sorry, Matron. Wrong envelope,' said Irene, and handed her another. Matron tore it open, and glared at Irene.

'Is this a joke? This is a dog's licence!'

'Gosh!' said Irene. 'So that's where old Rover's licence went! Sorry, Matron. *This* must be the right envelope!'

Everyone was giggling. Alicia had now joined the mob round Matron, her bright eyes enjoying the joke. Matron opened the third envelope. She began to laugh.

It was a cleverly drawn picture of herself scolding Irene for forgetting her health certificate. Belinda, Irene's friend, had drawn it, and the two of them had pushed it into the third envelope for a joke.

'I shall keep this as a memento of you, Irene,' said Matron. 'It shall be pinned up in my room as a warning to all girls who have bad memories. And now – what about the real thing, please?'

The 'real thing' was produced at last, and Matron pronounced herself satisfied. 'I suppose you *had* to keep up the tradition of losing your certificate for the last time,' she smiled. 'Now, June, where's yours – and you, Jo?'

Felicity came up and Darrell gave her her certificate to hand in. Then she went off with Alicia and Sally to see who was back.

'I bet that's Bill!' said Darrell, suddenly, as she caught the sound of horses' hooves up the drive. 'I wonder how many brothers are with her this time!'

Wilhelmina, Bill for short, had seven brothers, all of whom were mad on horses. Some of them accompanied her to school each term, which always caused a great sensation! The girls ran to the window to see.

'Yes – it's Bill – but there are only three brothers with her,' said Sally. 'I suppose that means another one's gone into the army, or into a job. Look, there's Clarissa too. She must have come with Bill on Merrylegs, her little horse.'

'*And* there's Gwen!' said Alicia, with malice in her voice. 'How many many fond farewells have we seen between Gwen and her mother? Let's feast our eyes on this one – it will be the last!'

But Gwen was on her guard now. Too often had the girls imitated her weeping farewells. She stepped out of the car, looking rather solemn, but very dignified. She kissed her mother and Miss Winter, her old governess, and wouldn't let them be silly over her. But she didn't kiss her father good-bye.

He called after her. 'Good-bye, Gwen.'

'Good-bye,' said Gwen, in such a hard voice that the girls looked at one another in surprise.

'There's been a row!' said Sally. 'I expect her father's ticked her off again for some silly nonsense. It's a jolly good thing for Gwendoline Mary that there's *one* sensible person in her family!'

Gwen's mother was now dabbing her eyes with her handkerchief. The car swung round, went down the drive and disappeared. Gwen came into the room behind the others.

'Hallo!' she said. 'Had good hols?'

'Hallo, Gwen,' said Darrell. 'Did you?'

'Fair,' said Gwen. 'My father was an awful nuisance, though.'

The others said nothing. Gwen never *could* understand that it just wasn't decent to run down your parents in public.

'Mother had fixed up for me to go to Switzerland to a simply marvellous finishing school,' said Gwen. 'Frightfully expensive. All the best people send their girls there. Lady Jane Tregennton's girl's going there, and . . .'

The same old Gwen! thought Darrell and Sally, feeling sick. Conceited, snobbish, silly. They turned away, feeling that nothing in the world would ever teach Gwen to be an ordinary decent, kindly girl.

Gwen didn't in the least mind talking to people's backs. She went on and on. 'And then, when it was all fixed, Dad said it was too expensive, and he said it was all nonsense, and I ought to get a job – a *job*! He said . . .'

'I don't think you ought to tell us all this,' said

Darrell, suddenly. 'I'm sure your father would hate it.'

'I don't care if he would or not,' said Gwen. 'He's tried to spoil everything. But I told him what I thought of him. I got my own way. I'm going!'

Sally looked at Darrell and Alicia. This was Gwen's last term. She had spent six years at Malory Towers, and had had many sharp lessons. Yet it seemed as if she had learned nothing of value at all!

She probably never will now, thought Darrell. It's too late. She walked out of the room with Sally and Alicia, all of them disgusted. Gwen scowled after them resentfully. People so often walked out on her, and she never could stop them.

Just as I was going to tell them some of the things I said to Dad, thought Gwen. I'm glad I hardly said good-bye to him. I'm his only daughter, and he treats me like that! Well, now he knows what I think of him.

She was so full of herself and her victory that she quite forgot to be mournful and homesick, as she usually pretended to be. She wandered off and found little Mary-Lou – a much bigger Mary-Lou now, but still shy and ready to think that most people were much better and more interesting than she was.

Mary-Lou always listened to everyone. Gwen began to tell her again all she had told the others. Mary-Lou stared at her in disgust. 'I don't believe you said anything *like* that to your father!' she said. 'You can't be as beastly as all *that*!'

And little Mary-Lou actually walked off with her nose in the air! Gwen suddenly began to realize that she wasn't going to be at all popular in her last term if she wasn't very very careful.

When supper-time came, the girls could see who was back and who wasn't. They could see the new girls in their Tower and they could see any new mistresses. Each Tower had its own common-rooms and dining-rooms. North Tower, where Darrell and her friends were, overlooked the sea, and was supposed to be the best Tower of all – though naturally the girls in the other Towers thought the same of theirs!

Darrell was sure there would be no new girls at all in the sixth. It was rare for a new girl to come so late to Malory Towers. She was very much surprised to see two new faces at the sixth-form table!

One girl was tall and sturdy and rather masculine looking, with her short cropped hair, and big legs and feet. The other was small, beautifully made, and had small hands and feet. As soon as she spoke, Darrell realized that she was French.

Mam'zelle Dupont introduced the girl, with one of her beaming smiles.

'Girls! This is Suzanne! She is niece to Mam'zelle Rougier who is in South Tower, but there is no room there for her, so she has come to me here. She will be in the sixth form – and she must learn the language well. Eh, Suzanne?'

'*Certainement*, Mam'zelle Dupont,' answered Suzanne, in a demure voice. She flashed a quick look round at the sixth-formers with bright black eyes, then lowered them again. Darrell felt a sudden liking for her.

'*Ah non* – you must not say one word of French, you bad girl!' scolded Mam'zelle. 'You must say "Certane-lee", not "*certainement*"!'

'Zer-tane-leee,' drawled Suzanne, and the girls laughed. Darrell nudged Sally.

'She's going to have some fun with Mam'zelle,' she said, in a low voice. 'And *we're* going to have some fun with Suzanne!'

3 Future plans

Mam'zelle then turned to the other new girl. 'And this is – how do you call yourself?' she asked the sturdy newcomer. 'Amanda Shoutalot?'

The girls laughed. The new girl gave Mam'zelle a rather contemptuous look. 'No – Amanda Chartelow,' she said, in a loud voice.

'Ah – that is what I said,' protested Mam'zelle. 'Amanda Shoutalot. Poor Amanda – her school has been burned down by fire! *Hélas* – it exists no longer!'

Nobody quite knew what to say. Amanda took some more bread, and ignored Mam'zelle. Gwen entered headlong into the gap in the conversation.

'Oh dear – what a dreadful thing! Did anyone get hurt?'

'No,' said Amanda, helping herself to more salad. 'It happened in the holidays. You probably read about it in the papers. It was Trenigan Towers.'

'Gosh, yes – I did read about it,' said Sally, remembering. 'Trenigan Towers! That's about the most

famous school for sport in the country, isn't it? I mean –
you win every single match you play, and you win all the
tennis shields and lacrosse cups?'

'That's right,' said Amanda. 'Well, it's gone. There
wasn't time to find another building in a hurry, so we all
had to scatter, and find other schools. I don't know how
long I'll be here – maybe a term, maybe longer. You
haven't much of a name for sport, have you, at Malory
Towers?'

This was rather too much from a new girl, even if she
had come into the sixth form, and had arrived from a
famous sports school. Darrell stared at her coldly.

'We're not too bad,' she said.

'Perhaps you'd like to give us a little coaching,' said
Alicia in the smooth voice that most of the girls
recognized as dangerous.

'I might,' said Amanda, and said no more. The girls
glanced at one another. Then they looked at Amanda and
saw how strong she must be. She was a great hefty girl
about five foot ten inches tall. How much did she weigh?

Must be thirteen stone, I should think! thought
Darrell, comparing Amanda with the slim, elegant French
girl. Goodness – have we got to put up with her all the
term? I shall find it hard to squash *her*!

Sally was thinking the same. She was games captain
for the whole school, a most important position. What
Sally said had to be taken notice of, from the sixth form
down to the first. Sally was a first-rate tennis player, a
first-rate lacrosse player, and one of the finest swimmers
Malory Towers had ever had. Nobody but Darrell could
beat her at tennis, and that very seldom.

She took another look at the stolid, rather scornful-looking Amanda. It was going to be very very difficult to give orders to her – especially as Amanda might easily prove to be a better tennis player and swimmer than even Sally herself. Sally was not as hefty as Amanda, though she was strong and supple.

'You were lucky to be able to find a place at Malory Towers,' gushed Gwen.

'Was I?' said Amanda, coldly, staring at Gwen as if she didn't like her at all. Gwen blinked. What a horrible girl! She hoped Alicia would be able to deal with her. Alicia could deal with anybody – her sharp tongue was quicker and more cutting than anyone else's in the school.

'I suppose you'll be going in for the Olympic Games,' said Alicia, meaning to be sarcastic. 'They're held next year in . . .'

'Oh yes. I should think I shall go in for about five different events,' said Amanda, calmly. 'My coach at Trenigan said I ought to win at least two.'

The girls gasped. Alicia looked taken aback. It had never entered her head that her scornful remark could be true. She looked so discomfited that Irene grinned.

'We ought to feel very honoured to have you here, Amanda!' she drawled.

'Thanks,' said Amanda, without looking at her.

'Amanda is such a beeg, beeg girl,' began Mam'zelle, mistaking Amanda's ungraciousness for shyness. 'She will be so marvellous at tennis. Sally, perhaps she will be in the Second Team, *n'est-ce pas*?'

Nobody replied to this. Sally merely grunted. Mam'zelle pushed on, under the impression that she was putting 'this great beeg Amanda' at her ease.

'How tall are you, Amanda?' she asked, feeling that

the girl must be at least seven feet tall; she had made plump little Mam'zelle feel so short when she had walked in beside her! 'And how many – er – how do you say it – how many pebbles do you weigh?'

There was a squeal of laughter from the table. Even Amanda deigned to smile. Mam'zelle gazed round indignantly.

'What have I said?' she demanded. 'Is it not right – pebbles?'

'No – *stones*, Mam'zelle,' chorused the girls, in delight. 'Our weight is measured by stones, not pebbles.'

'Stones – pebbles – they are the same,' said Mam'zelle. 'Never, never shall I learn this English language.'

The bell rang for the meal to end. All the girls got up, laughing. Dear old Mam'zelle – her mistakes would fill a book.

Darrell and her friends went up to her study to talk and gossip. There were the usual crowd – Sally, Alicia, Belinda, Irene, Mary-Lou, Bill and Clarissa. Mavis was not there.

'It seems strange without Mavis,' said Sally. 'She's gone to train as a singer now. Perhaps we shall all crowd into her concerts one day!'

'I miss quiet old Janet too,' said Darrell. 'She is training as a dress designer. She ought to be jolly good at it! Do you remember the marvellous dresses she made for us when we gave that pantomime in the fifth form?'

'Catherine has left too,' said Alicia. 'Thank goodness! I never knew such a door-mat in my life. No wonder we called her *Saint* Catherine!'

'She wasn't so bad,' said Mary-Lou, loyally. 'It was only that she did like doing things for people so much.'

'She did them in the wrong way, that's all,' said Bill. 'She always made herself such a martyr. What's she going to do?'

'She's going to stay at home and help Mama,' said Alicia, rather maliciously. 'It'll suit her down to the ground. Mama thinks herself a bit of an invalid, I gather – so Catherine will really enjoy herself, being a saintly little daughter.'

'Don't be unkind, Alicia,' said Mary-Lou. 'Catherine was kind underneath her door-mat ways.'

'I take your word for it,' said Alicia, smiling at Mary-Lou. 'Don't get all hot and bothered. This is only a good old gossip! What are *you* going to do when you leave next year, Mary-Lou?'

'I'm leaving sooner than that,' said Mary-Lou. 'I've made up my mind what I'm going to be, and I'm going off to train in September. I'm going to be a hospital nurse – a children's nurse. I never wanted to be anything else, really. I'm going to train at Great Ormond Street Hospital. It's all settled.'

The others looked at quiet, loyal, idealistic Mary-Lou. Immediately each one of them saw that she had chosen the right career for herself. Nursing was a vocation – something you felt you *had* to do, for the sake of other people. It was absolutely right for Mary-Lou.

'I can't imagine anything you'd love better, Mary-Lou!' said Darrell, warmly. 'It's exactly right for you, and *you're* exactly right for it! Lucky children who have you to nurse them!'

Mary-Lou looked pleased and embarrassed. She looked round at the others. 'What are we all going to do?' she said. 'Belinda's easy, of course.'

18

'Yes. I've *got* to be an artist,' said Belinda. 'I always knew that. It's easy, of course, when you've got a gift. You can't do anything else but use it.'

'And Irene will study music,' said Sally. 'That's easy too. Bill – what about you – and Clarissa? You are both so mad on horses that I can't imagine you taking a job unless it's on horseback.'

Clarissa looked at Bill. She grinned. 'You've hit the nail on the head,' she said. 'Our job *will* be on horseback. Won't it, Bill?'

Bill nodded. 'Yes. Clarissa and I are going to run a riding school together.'

'You're not!' exclaimed the others, amazed and interested.

'Yes, we are. We decided it last hols,' explained Clarissa. 'I was staying with Bill, and we heard there were some stables for sale. We thought we'd like to get them, take our own horses, buy a few more, and begin a riding school. Actually it's not very far from here. We did wonder if we could get Miss Grayling to let us have some Malory Towers girls for pupils.'

'*Well*!' said Alicia, in deep admiration. 'If you two aren't dark horses!'

There was a yell of laughter at this typical Alicia joke. Bill grinned. She never said very much but she was a most determined young person. Nobody had any doubt at all but that the Bill–Clarissa riding school would be very successful indeed.

'I'll see that all my children are your pupils, when they come to Malory Towers,' promised Alicia, with a grin. 'Fancy you two thinking all this out and never saying a word!'

There was a short silence. It seemed as if most of them knew what they were going to do when they left school – and had chosen rightly.

'Well, Sally and I are going to college,' said Darrell. 'And so is Alicia – and Betty is coming too. We're all going to St Andrews up in Scotland, and what a good time we'll have!'

'You'll feel funny at first – being the youngest again, instead of the oldest,' said Belinda. 'I suppose you'll take Arts, Darrell, and eventually be a writer?'

'I don't know,' said Darrell. 'It's what I'd like to be. But, you see, Sally and I are not as lucky as you and Irene, Belinda. We haven't a gift that sticks out a mile – or a vocation like Mary-Lou. We've got to find what we're best fitted for, and we can do that at the University. We'll jolly well have to use our brains there, too. We'll be up against some brilliant people.'

Sally got up. 'Where did we put those biscuits, Darrell?' she said. 'Talking always makes me hungry. That's one thing that still makes me think we're not really very grown-up, even though we sometimes think we're getting on that way – we always feel so *hungry*. Grown-ups never seem to feel like that!'

'Long live our appetites!' said Alicia, taking a biscuit. 'And may our shadows never grow less!'

4 In Miss Grayling's room

Next day everyone awoke to the sound of the loud clang of the dressing-bell. New girls sat up in bed, startled, unused to the loud morning bell. Second-formers grunted and rolled over for another snooze. They were a notoriously lazy form that year. Darrell was always teasing her second-form sister, Felicity, about it.

'Lazy lot of kids,' she said. 'Always rushing down to breakfast with your ties half-knotted and your shoes undone. I wonder Miss Parker doesn't deal out punishments by the hundred!'

'Oh, old Nosey does!' grinned Felicity. 'Was she as bad in your time, Darrell, always nosing into this and that?'

'Never you mind,' said Darrell, remembering how she herself as a second-former had scrambled down to breakfast once with only one stocking on. 'How's that awful Josephine getting on?'

'Oh, throwing her weight about as usual,' said Felicity. 'Susan and I don't take much notice of her. It's when she comes up against June that she gets it hot! June simply *pulverizes* her! Serves her right.'

Darrell was quite sure that June would be able to 'pulverize' anyone, as Felicity called it. June was Alicia's young cousin, a very tough and aggressive young person, only slightly mellowed so far by her stay at Malory Towers. She was very like Alicia, and had Alicia's quick tongue and sharp humour. She also had Alicia's love of tricks, and everyone who taught her had learned to keep a very sharp eye indeed on June.

Except Mam'zelle Dupont! Anyone could play a joke on her and get away with it. But it was getting more difficult now, since Mam'zelle had discovered that there were actually booklets and leaflets sent out by firms, describing their jokes and tricks. She had made an intensive study of these, and was now much more on the alert.

'Do you remember when Mam'zelle played a trick on *us*?' said Felicity, giggling as she remembered. 'She bought a set of false celluloid teeth and fitted them over her own – do you remember? And everyone she smiled at had a fit, she looked so monstrous!'

'Yes, I shall never forget,' said Darrell. 'Dear old Mam'zelle. I do wish she'd play a "treek" this last term. That's her one and only so far.'

One or two girls still hadn't come back, because of illness or some good reason. Moira in the sixth form was due back that day. She and Sally worked well together over the games time-tables and matches – but otherwise Moira was still not very likeable.

'She's always so jolly sure of herself – so determined to be cock-of-the-walk!' complained the girls. 'Never in the wrong, mustn't be contradicted – the great high-and-mighty Moira!'

Darrell caught sight of Amanda, the new sixth-former, going past. Something in the determined, confident walk reminded her of Moira. She smiled to herself.

'How will Moira like Amanda? It'll be funny to watch them together. There'll be some battles this term! Well –

it's always more interesting when things happen. I wouldn't want my very last term to be dull.'

She went to the common-room after breakfast to find the others in her form. Sally was there, and Mary-Lou and Belinda.

'The bell for the first class will soon go,' said Darrell. 'I suppose we'd better go down.'

Someone knocked at the door. 'Come in!' called Darrell. A scared-looking second-former put her nose round the door. 'Please,' she began.

'Come *right* in,' said Belinda. 'We like to know the face has got a body. We shan't eat you!'

The second-former inserted her body into the room too. 'Please,' she said, 'Miss Grayling says will one of you take the new girls to her. She says not the new sixth-former, but any others in North Tower. She's waiting now.'

'Right,' said Darrell. 'Buzz off. Are the girls waiting in the hall, as usual?'

'Yes, please,' said the scared one, and buzzed off thankfully.

'I'll take the kids in,' said Mary-Lou, getting up. New girls always had to go to the Head on the morning of the second day. Miss Grayling liked to give them an idea of what was expected of them at Malory Towers and, as a rule, no girl forgot those few grave words. Darrell had never forgotten them.

She remembered them now and suddenly put out a hand to stop Mary-Lou.

'Mary-Lou – let *me* take them in. It's my job, anyway – and I just feel I'd somehow like to hear Miss Grayling talk to the new girls as she once talked to us. *I'll* go!'

'Right,' said Mary-Lou, understanding at once. She sat down again. Darrell went out of the room and into the hall. The new girls were there, five of them. Three were first-formers, one was a second-former and one a third-former. They all looked uncomfortable and rather scared.

'It's the head-girl!' hissed the third-former. 'Mind your Ps and Qs.'

Nobody had any intention of not minding them. The little first-formers looked with wide eyes at this big, important sixth-former. Darrell remembered how scared she had been of sixth-formers too, six years back, and she smiled kindly at them.

'Come along, kids. I'll take you in. Don't look so scared. You've come to the finest school in the world, so you're lucky!'

Darrell took the five girls to the Head Mistress's room, and stopped outside a door painted a deep cream colour. She knocked.

A low, familiar voice called out, 'Come in!'

Darrell opened the door. 'I've brought the new girls to you, Miss Grayling,' she said.

'Thank you, Darrell,' said the Head. She was sitting at her desk, writing, a grey-haired, calm-faced woman, with startlingly blue eyes and a determined mouth. She looked at the five trembling girls standing in front of her, her blue eyes going from one to the other, considering each girl closely.

What did she see in them? Darrell wondered. Did she see the bad – and the good? Did she see which girls could be trusted and which couldn't? Did she know which of them would accept responsibility and do well in the school, and which would be failures?

Miss Grayling spoke to each girl in her low, clear voice, asking their names and forms. Then she addressed them all gravely. Darrell listened as intently as the youngsters, remembering the words from six years back.

'I want you all to listen to me for a minute or two. One day you will leave this school and go out into the world as young women. You should take with you eager minds, kind hearts and a will to help. You should take with you a good understanding of many things and a willingness to accept responsibility, and show yourselves as women to be loved and trusted. All these things you will be able to learn at Malory Towers – if you *will*.'

She paused, and every girl looked at her intently, listening hard.

'I do not count as our successes those who have won scholarships and passed exams, though these are good things to do. I count as our successes those who learn to be good-hearted and kind, sensible and trustable, good, sound women the world can lean on. Our failures are those who do not learn these things in the years they are here.'

Darrell wished she could see into the faces of the five listening girls. What were they thinking, these new-comers? Were they making up their minds, as she had once done, that they would each be one of Malory Towers' successes? The five girls hardly breathed as they gazed at Miss Grayling and listened.

'Some of you will find it easy to learn these things, others will find it hard,' went on Miss Grayling. 'But, easy or hard, they must be learned if you are to be happy after you leave here, and if you are to bring happiness to others.'

Miss Grayling stopped. She looked across at Darrell, who was listening with as much attention as the youngsters.

'Darrell,' said Miss Grayling. 'Do you remember my saying these words to you, when you first came here?'

'Yes, Miss Grayling,' said Darrell. 'And you said something else too. You said, "You will all get a tremendous lot out of your time at Malory Towers. See that you give a lot back." '

'I did say that,' said Miss Grayling. 'And now I must add to it. Girls, six years ago I said those words to Darrell. She is one who *has* got a great deal out of her time here – and there is no one who has given more back than Darrell has.'

The five girls looked in awe at Darrell, their head-girl. They couldn't imagine her standing as a twelve-year-old in front of Miss Grayling, hearing those same words. But Miss Grayling remembered very well.

'You may go,' said the Head, pleased with the look of the five new girls. They were good stuff, she thought – likely to be the heads of forms and captains of games – and possibly head-girls of the future.

Darrell turned to go too. 'Wait a moment, Darrell,' said Miss Grayling. 'Shut the door.'

Darrell shut the door and came back to the desk. She felt herself blushing, she had been so pleased at Miss Grayling's words about her. She looked shyly at the Head.

'You are one of our successes, Darrell,' said Miss Grayling. 'One of our biggest successes. Sally is another, and so is Mary-Lou. I think there is only one sad failure, *real* failure, in your form. And she has only this one term to change herself. You know who it is I mean.'

'Yes,' said Darrell. 'Gwendoline.'

Miss Grayling sighed. 'You know her perhaps better than I do,' she said. 'Can you do anything with her at all? I have had a most unpleasant interview these holidays with Gwendoline's parents about her future. Her mother wanted one thing, her father another. Her father, of course, is right. But I hear that he has had to give way in the matter. Darrell, if you possibly can, I want you to try and influence Gwendoline so that she will come round to her father's point of view. Otherwise the family will be split in half, and there will be great unhappiness.'

'I'll try,' said Darrell, but so doubtfully that Miss Grayling knew there was little hope of success. 'I know all about it, of course, Miss Grayling – Gwen has seen to that! But it's impossible to move Gwen when she's determined to get her own way.'

'Well, never mind,' said the Head, smiling suddenly. 'I can put up with twenty Gwens so long as I have a few Sallys and Darrells!'

5 In Miss Oakes's class

Darrell went out of the room, feeling so proud and pleased that she could have sung out loud. She was one of the successes! She had always longed to be – but she had made mistakes, been unkind sometimes, lost her temper more times than she liked to remember – and had ruefully come to the conclusion that although she wasn't a failure, she wasn't a howling success either.

But Miss Grayling seemed to think she was, so she must be. Darrell held her head high, and went swinging along to the sixth-form classroom. She opened the door and went in quietly.

'I'm sorry I'm late, Miss Oakes,' she said. 'I took the new girls to Miss Grayling.'

'Yes, Mary-Lou told me,' said Miss Oakes. 'We were just talking about the work this term, Darrell. Those of you who are taking Higher Certificate are to work in one group, taking only a few odd lessons with the rest of the form. You have been working hard for the last two terms, so you should not find this term unduly hard – but you will have to keep at it!' Darrell nodded. She badly wanted to pass the Higher well. She felt sure Sally would. As for Alicia and Betty, their quick brains and excellent memories would make success certain. She glanced round at the other girls from the other Towers, who would also be taking Higher. Yes – they would probably all pass. They were a keen, hard-working lot.

'I'm glad *I'm* not taking Higher,' said Gwen. 'Anyway, I suppose I could always take it at my school in Switzerland, couldn't I, Miss Oakes?'

Miss Oakes was not interested in Gwen's future school, any more than she was interested in Gwen.

'You are not up to Higher standard, whatever school you happen to be in,' she said coldly. 'I can only hope that you will work a little better this term than you have worked for the last two terms, Gwendoline. Would it be too difficult to leave me with a little better impression of your capabilities than I have at present?'

Gwen squirmed. She looked round at Maureen for sympathy. She got none, for Maureen always delighted in seeing Gwen made uncomfortable. The others looked studiously into the distance, determined not to catch Gwen's eye or give her any chance of speaking about her future school. They felt certain they were going to get very very tired of hearing about it.

'Amanda, I understand that you were going to work for Higher, if your old school had not been destroyed,' said Miss Oakes, turning to the hefty, solid new girl. 'Do you wish to do so here? I hear that it has been left to you to decide, as you can take it next year if you want to?'

'I don't want to take it this term, thank you,' said Amanda. 'It would be muddling, having had the work with different teachers. I shouldn't do myself justice. I intend to work at my games instead. I hope to be chosen for the Olympic Games next year, anyway.'

Only the North Tower girls had heard this bit of news so far. The girls from other Towers gaped at Amanda's forthright assertion. Go in for the *Olympic Games*! She must either be mad, or else alarmingly good at games!

'Ah yes,' said Miss Oakes, calmly. 'I forgot you came from Trenigan Towers. Well, Amanda, you will find that the games side is very good here, fortunately for you – and very well run.'

Amanda looked disbelieving, but didn't say anything. It was, however, quite apparent to everyone that she was busy turning up her rather big nose at the games she might expect at Malory Towers. Sally felt annoyed and half-amused. Moira felt angry. She glared at Amanda, making up her mind to take her down a few pegs as quickly as possible!

And if she tries to interfere, I'll soon show that *I* don't stand any nonsense, even if Sally does! thought Moira, scowling so fiercely at her thoughts that Belinda's hand went instinctively into her desk for her sketch-book – the one the girls called her Scowl Book. It had a most wonderful collection of scowls – though the finest were undoubtedly Gwen's!

How Gwen wished she could get hold of that horrible book of Belinda's! But Belinda guarded it jealously and had such a fine hiding-place for it when she took it out of her desk that Gwen had never been able to make out where it was.

'No, Belinda,' said Miss Oakes, who had already learned to recognize the Scowl Book when she saw it. 'We will have no Scowl Sketches in this session, please. And, Irene, could you stop tapping out that tune, whatever it is, on your desk?'

'Oh sorry,' said Irene, stopping the tapping at once. 'I just can't help it when a new tune comes into my head. It's the way the wind blows in those trees over there, Miss Oakes – shusha, shusha, shusha – like that, it goes. And it made me . . .'

'You're tapping *again*, Irene,' said Miss Oakes, impatiently. She was never quite certain if Irene really *did* get as lost in her 'tunes' as she said she did, or if she acted like this to make a diversion and cause laughter.

But Irene was quite serious about it. She lived half in a world of music and half in the world of ordinary things – and when one world clashed with the other, she was lost! She was quite capable of writing out a tune in

French *Dictée* instead of a word of French – and quite capable, too, of handing it in! Mam'zelle had often been amazed to find herself staring at pages of music notes, instead of lists of French verbs.

The French girl, Suzanne, had sat with her eyes half closed through the talk so far. Miss Oakes spoke to her suddenly and made her jump.

'Suzanne! Are you listening?'

'Police?' said Suzanne. Miss Oakes looked surprised.

'She means "Please?" ' said Darrell, with a laugh. 'She *keeps* saying "Police?" whenever she doesn't understand anything. Don't you, Suzanne?'

'Police?' said Suzanne, not understanding a word. 'Police, Darrell, *je ne comprends pas*. I not unnerstand!'

'Well, Suzanne, you will have to listen with your ears *and* eyes open,' said Miss Oakes, 'or you will not learn a word of English while you are here. I understand that is why you have come – to learn to speak English fluently?'

'Police?' repeated Suzanne, again, her black eyes very wide open. 'I spik him bad.'

'What *does* she mean?' said Miss Oakes.

'She means she speaks English badly,' said Sally.

'She must have special coaching then,' said Miss Oakes, firmly.

'No, no. I not want zat,' said Suzanne, equally firmly.

'Ah – so you understood what I said *then*,' said Miss Oakes, beginning to be suspicious of this innocent-looking Suzanne.

'Police?' said Suzanne again, and Miss Oakes gave it up. She privately resolved to have a few words with Mam'zelle Rougier about her seemingly stupid niece. She began to give out instructions regarding the work to be done that term, what books were to be used, and what work was to be done by the girls on their own.

'I like old Oakey,' said Darrell, at break. 'But I've often wished she had more sense of humour. She never, never, never sees a joke. But she always *suspects* there may be somebody leading her up the garden path.'

'Yes. Like Irene and her tunes,' said Belinda, 'and actually Irene is perfectly serious about them. Look at her now – shusha, shush, shusha, shush, over by the window, with her eyes glued on the trees.'

Alicia grinned wickedly. She went up to Irene and tapped her on the shoulder. 'I say, Irene – can I play trains too? Shush, shusha, shush, shusha – come on, let's play trains.'

And before the surprised Irene knew what was happening, half the sixth-formers had formed a line and were playing 'trains' behind Irene, chuffing like engines.

Amanda watched disdainfully. What a school! she thought. Now if she were at Trenigan Towers, everyone would be out practising tennis strokes or something!

'Hold it, Amanda, hold it!' said Belinda, suddenly, spotting the unpleasant look on Amanda's large face. She had whipped out her Scowl Book, and was busy drawing. Amanda had no idea what she was doing. She was so new that she didn't even realize that Belinda could draw.

She saw in horror that Belinda had caught her face and expression exactly. She snatched at the book but Belinda dodged out of the way.

'I *didn't* look like that,' said Amanda, enraged. 'I just stood there thinking that if I were at my old school, we wouldn't be playing the fool like this, but out in the open air, practising strokes at tennis, or something sensible.'

'Really?' said Moira, coldly. 'I suppose it has escaped your notice that at the moment it is pelting with rain?'

Actually Amanda *hadn't* noticed. She had been too busy scorning the others at their fooling. She turned away, after giving Moira a most unpleasant look which Moira fully returned. Darrell thought there wasn't a pin to choose between the two looks!

Amanda turned off to the corner where the radio stood. She began to fiddle about with it and eventually managed to find a recording of some sporting event. The commentator was very excited, and his voice came loudly through the common-room, where the girls were having their break.

Nobody quite liked to tell her to turn it down a bit. Darrell nudged Sally and nodded to the window. It had stopped raining. Sally grinned.

She and Darrell made signs to the others to creep out of the room without disturbing Amanda. One by one they tiptoed out, and Darrell softly closed the door. They rushed to the cloakroom, found their lockers, slipped on tennis shoes, snatched up their rackets and ran out to the courts.

'Let's hope she sees us!' panted Moira.

Amanda did. The recording came to an end and she switched off the radio. She was immediately struck by the quiet in the room, and swung round. It was empty. She heard the sound of voices outside, and the thud of tennis balls being struck, and went to the window. She scowled down. Beasts! They were just doing all that to annoy her!

The girls came back, laughing, when the bell went.

'Pity you didn't feel like a practice, Amanda!' called Moira. 'Never mind – better luck next time!'

6 Down in the pool

As usual the girls settled down very quickly for the new term. The summer term was always such a lovely one. There were so many things to do – and for those who liked swimming, the magnificent pool that lay in a great hollow of a rock down below on the shore was a source of the greatest delight.

Those who wished could go to swim before breakfast, and every morning, once the pool had been declared warm enough for swimming, girls ran down the steep cliff-path to the swimming-pool. They wore their swimming-costumes with a wrap round them.

Most of the girls loved the pool. A few didn't. Those who hadn't learned to swim were afraid. Those who didn't like cold water hated the pool. Gwen, of course, was one of these, and so was Maureen.

The new French girl also hated the very idea of the pool. She went to watch the girls there once, and squealed in fright if a splash of water so much as reached her toes!

'Suzanne! Don't be an idiot!' said Miss Potts, who happened to be in charge of the swimming that day. 'If you squeal like a silly first-former I shall make you strip off your clothes and go in. I can't think why Mam'zelle doesn't make you.'

Mam'zelle, of course, never would make anyone go into the pool if they didn't want to. She detested it herself, and so did the second French teacher, Mam'zelle Rougier, Suzanne's aunt. Neither of them understood the craze for games and sports of all kinds that they found in English schools.

'I go back,' announced Suzanne, at the next splash, and she turned to go up the sloping way to the cliff on which the school was built.

'Oh no, you don't,' said Miss Potts. 'You stay here. Even if you can't be persuaded to learn to swim, you can watch the others!'

'Police?' said Suzanne, with a blank expression on her face. Miss Potts wished fervently she had Suzanne in the first form under her for just one day. She was quite certain that Suzanne would never utter that infuriating word again!

Gwendoline and Maureen were made to swim, of course, though it still took them ages to make up their minds to get into the cold, clear water. They waited till everyone else was in, because it was simply extraordinary how many accidental pushes happened to them when Alicia or Moira or Betty came by. If there was one thing Gwen hated it was to enter the pool suddenly without warning!

The pool was always beautiful on blue sunny days. It shone a deeper blue than the sky, and after a few weeks of summer got really deliciously warm – till the tide came in, swamped the pool, and left cooler water there! Darrell loved the pool. Even when she was not swimming she used to take her books down beside it and dream there, looking over the brilliant blue water.

Moira was a very good swimmer. So was Sally. Darrell always had been. But the new girl, Amanda, surpassed them all!

She was a most magnificent swimmer. The first time she entered the water, everyone gasped. She streaked across the pool with the most powerful over-arm stroke the girls had ever seen.

'Gosh – what a swimmer!' said Darrell. 'I never saw anything like it. She *is* good enough for the Olympic Games. She could beat us hollow, Sally.'

Amanda was not content with the pool, big and deep though it was. She looked out to sea. 'I shall go and swim in the sea,' she said.

'You're not allowed to,' said Darrell, who was nearby, drying herself. 'There's a very dangerous current out there at high tide.'

'Currents aren't dangerous to a strong swimmer like me,' said Amanda, and flexed her arms to show Darrell her enormous muscles. She had great strong legs too. She was heavy in her walk, and not at all graceful in ordinary life – but when she was playing games or swimming, she had the strong grace of some big animal, and was most fascinating to watch. The lower forms gaped at her, and often came down to the pool when the word went round that Amanda was there – just to stand and stare!

'Would you like to give some of these youngsters a bit of coaching, Amanda?' Sally said one day. As head of school games, she was always on the look-out for likely youngsters to coach.

'I might,' said Amanda, looking bored. 'So long as it's not a waste of my time.'

'Oh well, if you feel like *that*!' said Moira indignantly. She was nearby, listening. Moira was not very likeable, but at least she did try to help the lower forms in their games, and was a great help to Sally.

'We never had to bother with the young ones at Trenigan Towers,' said Amanda, drying herself so vigorously that her skin came up bright red. 'We had plenty of coaches there. *They* looked after the youngsters. You seem to have too few games mistresses here.'

Darrell fumed inwardly at this criticism of Malory Towers. There were plenty of teachers for everything! Just because Malory Towers didn't make a religion of sport as Trenigan had, this great lump of an Amanda dared to look down her nose at it!

Sally saw Darrell's face, and nudged her. 'It's no good saying anything,' she said, as Amanda walked off. 'She's so thick-skinned, and so sure of herself and her future, that nothing we can say will make any impression. She must have been very upset when Trenigan went up in smoke – and she probably hates Malory Towers because it's new to her, and doesn't go in for the sport she adores as much as she'd like it to!'

'She's jolly lucky to *come* here,' snorted Darrell, still looking furious. Sally laughed. It was a long time since she had seen Darrell near to losing her famous temper. Once upon a time Darrell had lost her temper practically every term and had shocked the school by her rages – but now it very seldom showed, for Darrell had it well under control.

'Don't let her get under your skin,' said Sally. 'Believe

me, she's much more likely to get under mine! She's infuriating over tennis – doesn't seem to think it's worth while even to have a game with us! She's got under Moira's skin all right – there'll be high words there soon.'

The second-formers came running down to the pool for their swim. The bigger girls heard the soft thud-thud of the rubber-shoed feet coming along, and turned. There was a yell from Felicity.

'Hallo, Darrell! Had a swim? What's the water like? Doesn't it look heavenly?'

'Wizard,' said Susan, her friend, and tried it with her toe as soon as she had taken off her shoes. 'Gosh, it's warming up already. Buck up, Felicity. The sooner we're in, the longer we'll have!'

Darrell had a few minutes to spare, and she stayed with Sally and Moira to watch the younger ones. Now that Darrell was so soon leaving, she felt an intense desire to make sure that there were others who would carry on worthily the great traditions of Malory Towers – and in particular she wanted to be sure that Felicity, her sister, would.

She watched Felicity with pride. She and Susan dived in quickly, and with strong, graceful strokes swam across the great pool and back.

'That sister of yours is coming on,' said Moira to Darrell. 'She was good last year – she's going to be even better this. I think if she improves her back stroke, we might try her in one of the teams.'

'I hope so,' said Darrell, longing for Felicity to shine. 'Susan's good too – but not nearly so fast. Hallo – who's this porpoise?'

A fat and ungainly girl stood shivering on the brink of the pool. She was yelled at by some of the second-formers already in the water.

'Get in, Jo! Come on, Fatty! If you don't buck up, you'll have exactly two minutes in the water, and that's all!'

Even two minutes was too much for the fat and cowardly Jo. Bumptious and brazen in everything else, she was a coward over cold water. She had begged her father to get her excused from swimming, and he had rung up Miss Grayling and informed her that he didn't wish his daughter Jo to go in for swimming if she didn't want to.

'Why not?' asked Miss Grayling, coldly. 'Has the doctor forbidden it for her?'

'No. But *I* have,' said the loud-voiced Mr. Jones, bellowing down the telephone. 'That's good enough, isn't it?'

'I'm afraid not,' said Miss Grayling, in her firm, decisive voice. 'Girls sent to Malory Towers follow the ordinary routine of the school, unless it is against doctor's orders. There is nothing wrong about swimming for Jo – she is merely afraid of cold water, so the games mistress tells me. I think you will agree with me that Josephine should conquer the cold water rather than that the cold water should defeat Josephine?'

Mr. Jones had been about to say that *he* had always detested cold water, and he didn't see why Jo shouldn't do what he had done, and not go near it; but he suddenly thought better of it. There was something in Miss Grayling's cool voice that warned him. He put down the telephone abruptly. Miss Grayling might find there was no room for Jo at Malory Towers, if he persisted!

And so Jo, to her annoyance and surprise, had been told by her father that she'd got to put up with the swimming and get on with it. Every day she had to come down to the pool and shiver in dread on the brink, till she was inevitably pushed in or dragged in by a scornful second-former. Even the first-formers had been known to push Jo in!

Today it was Felicity who crept up behind, gave Jo an enormous shove, and landed her in the pool with a colossal splash! Jo came up, gasping and spluttering, furiously angry. When she had got the water out of her mouth, she turned on the laughing Felicity.

'You beast! That's the second time you've done that. Just you wait, I'll pay you out. You're as bad as your father!'

'What's my father done?' asked Felicity, amused.

'He was rude to mine,' said Jo. 'About pushing your car into the hedge. *I* heard him!'

'Oh well – he pushed our car into the hedge – and now I've pushed you into the water!' cried Felicity. 'Tit for tat! We're quits! Look out – I'm coming to duck you!'

She dived under the water to get Jo's legs. Jo screamed and kicked. Her legs slid away from her and she disappeared under the water again. She came up, furious. She struggled to the side and called to Sally.

'Sally! Can't you stop Felicity playing the fool in the water? She's always going for my legs.'

'Learn to swim then,' said Sally. 'Get some coaching! You always slip out of any coaching. Look out – here comes somebody else after your legs!'

Poor Jo! However much she swaggered and boasted and blew her own trumpet out of the water, she was of less account than the youngest first-former when she was in the pool!

7   Darrell and Gwen

Darrell hoped that her last term would go very very slowly. So did Sally.

'I want to hold on to every moment, this last term,' said Darrell. 'I know quite well we'll have a wonderful time at St Andrews, when we leave here – but I do so love Malory Towers, and I want the time to go as slowly as possible. I want to go away remembering every detail of it. I never want to forget.'

'Well, we shall remember all the things we want to remember,' said Sally. 'We shall remember all the tricks we've ever played on Mam'zelle, for instance – every single one! We shall remember how the pool looks on a sunny day – and how the sea looks from the classroom windows – and what it sounds like when the girls pour out of school at the end of the morning.'

'And you'll remember dear Gwen and her ways,' said Alicia, who was nearby. 'You'll never forget those!'

'Oh, *Gwen*!' said Darrell, exasperated at the thought of her. 'I wouldn't mind forgetting every single thing about her. She's spoiling our last term with her silly behaviour!'

Gwen really was being very trying. She had never liked Malory Towers, because she had never fitted in with its ideas and ideals. She was spoiled, selfish and silly, and yet thought herself a most attractive and desirable person. The only other girl in the form at all like her, Maureen, she detested. She could see that Maureen *was* like her in many many ways, and she didn't like seeing herself so often in a girl she disliked.

Gwen never stopped talking about her next and last school. 'It's in Switzerland, you know,' she said a hundred times. '*The* best school there. It's called a finishing school, and is very very select.'

'Well, I hope it will finish you off properly,' said Alicia. 'It's time something put an end to you!'

'That's not funny, Alicia,' said Gwen, looking dignified. 'Very first-formish.'

'You always *make* me feel first-formish,' said Alicia. 'I think of silly things like putting out my tongue and saying "Yah!" when you start talking about your idiotic school. Why you couldn't have gone this term, and left us to enjoy our last term in peace, I simply can't imagine.'

'I had an awful fight to go,' said Gwen, and the others groaned. They had already heard far too often about Gwen's 'fight'. Each time she told them, she related worse and worse things that she had said to her father.

'I bet she didn't say half those things,' said Alicia to Darrell. 'No father would stand it – and Mr. Lacy has put Gwen in her place plenty of times before!'

However, it was true that Gwen had said some very cruel things to her father during the last holidays, backed up by her mother. Mrs. Lacy had been so set on sending Gwen to a finishing school where she could 'make nice friends', that she had used every single means in her power to back Gwen up.

Tears and more tears. Reproaches. Sulks. Cruel words. Mrs. Lacy had brought them all out, and Gwen added to them. The old governess, Miss Winter, who adored Gwen and thought the world of Mrs. Lacy, had been shocked.

Gwen related it all to her unwilling listeners. 'Miss Winter was an idiot. All she could say was, "Your father is tired, Gwendoline. He's not been well for some time. Don't you think it would be better not to worry him so much?" She's silly and weak – always has been.'

'Shut up,' said Sally. 'I'd hate to treat my father like that.'

'I said to my father, "Aren't I your only daughter? Do you grudge me one more year's happiness?" ' went on Gwen, throwing herself into the part with all her heart. 'I said, "You don't love me. You never did! If you did, you would let me have this one small thing I want – that Mother wants too." '

'I said, shut up,' said Sally, again. 'We don't want to hear this. It doesn't reflect any credit on you, Gwen. It's beastly.'

'Oh, you're rather a prig, Sally, aren't you?' said Gwen, with her little affected laugh. 'Anyway, you wouldn't have the courage to stand up to your father, I'm sure.'

'You don't have to "stand up" to your parents if you pull together,' said Sally, shortly.

'Do go on, Gwen,' said Maureen, from her corner of the room. 'It's so interesting. You sound so grown-up!'

Gwen was surprised at this tribute from Maureen,

but very pleased. She didn't see that Maureen was encouraging her to go on simply so that she might make herself a nuisance and a bore to everyone. Maureen could see how disgusted the others were. She was rather disgusted herself. Although she was very like Gwen, she did at least love her parents.

Let Gwen go on and on! she thought. Horrid creature! She's showing herself up properly!

And so Gwen went on, talking to Maureen, repeating the unkind things she had said to her father, exulting in the victory she had won over him.

'I went on till I got my way,' she said. 'I stayed in bed one whole day and Mother told him I'd be really ill if I went on like that. So Daddy came upstairs and said, "Very well. You can have your way. You're right and I'm wrong. You can go to Switzerland to school." '

Nobody believed that her father had said this. Nobody said anything at all except Maureen.

'What a victory, Gwendoline,' she said. 'I bet you were all over your father after that.'

'I would have been if he'd have let me,' said Gwen, looking a little puzzled. 'But he went all grieved and sad, and hardly spoke to any of us. Except sometimes to Miss Winter. He was putting it on, of course, to make me feel awful. But I didn't. Two can play at that game, I thought, so I went cool too. I hardly even said good-bye to him when he drove the car away at the beginning of term. You've *got* to stand up to your parents when you get to our age!'

Darrell stood up suddenly. She felt really sick. She thought of her own father, Mr. Rivers – kindly, hard-working surgeon, devoted to his wife and two daughters.

How would he feel if she, Darrell, suddenly 'stood up' to him, and spoke cruel words, as Gwen had to her father?

He'd be heart-broken! thought Darrell. And I'm sure Mr. Lacy felt the same. I expect he loves Gwen, even if she is beastly and selfish. How *could* she behave like that?

She spoke to Gwen, and the tone of her voice made everyone look up.

'Gwen, I'd like a few words with you,' said Darrell. 'Come on up to my study, will you?'

Gwen was surprised. What did Darrell want with her? She felt like refusing, and then got up. She was rather afraid of the forthright Darrell.

Darrell led the way to her study. She had remembered Miss Grayling's words. Could she possibly say something now, this very minute, to influence Gwen, and show her where she had gone wrong? Darrell felt that she might. She felt so strongly about the matter that she was certain she could make Gwen see her point.

'Sit down in that arm-chair, Gwen,' said Darrell. 'I want to say something to you.'

'I hope you're not going to preach at me,' said Gwen. 'You've got on that kind of face.'

'Well, I'm not going to preach,' said Darrell, hoping that she wasn't. 'Look here, Gwen – I can't help feeling terribly sorry for your father about all this.'

Gwen was amazed. 'Sorry for my *father*! Why? What's it to do with you, anyway?'

'Well, you've told us so often about this family row of yours, that I, for one, can't help feeling that it *is* something to do with me now,' said Darrell. 'I mean – you've made me share in all that bickering and rows and upsets, and I feel almost as if I've been a spectator.'

Gwen was silent for once. Darrell went on.

'I'm not going to say a word about who's right or who's wrong, Gwen,' said Darrell, earnestly. 'I'm not going to criticize anyone. I just say this. From what you've told me you've made that nice father of yours miserable. You've got what you want at the expense of someone else's peace of mind.'

'I've got to stand on my own feet, haven't I?' muttered Gwen.

'Not if you stamp on someone else's toes to do it,' said Darrell, warming up. 'Don't you love your father, Gwen? I couldn't possibly treat mine as you've treated yours. If you did say all those cruel things to yours, then you ought to say you're sorry.'

'I'm not sorry I said them,' said Gwen, in a hard voice. 'My father's often said unkind things to me.'

'Well, *you* deserved them,' said Darrell, beginning to lose patience. 'He doesn't. I've met him plenty of times and I think he's a dear. You don't deserve a father like that!'

'You said you weren't going to preach,' said Gwen, scornfully. 'How long are you going on like this?'

Darrell looked at Gwen's silly, weak face and marvelled that such a weak person could be so hard and unyielding. She tried once again, though she now felt sure that it was no use. Nobody in this world could make any impression on Gwen!

'Gwen,' she began. 'You said that your father said he couldn't *afford* to send you to Switzerland. If so, he'll have to go short of something himself, to let you go.'

'He was wrong when he said he couldn't afford it,'

said Gwen. 'Mother said he could. He was just saying that as an excuse not to let me go. He was horrid about the whole thing. He said – he said – that I was s-s-silly enough without being made s-s-s-sillier, and that a good j-j-job would shake me out of a lot of n-n-nonsense!'

Stuttering with self-pity, Gwen now dissolved into tears. Darrell looked at her in despair.

'Couldn't you possibly go to your father and say you're sorry, you'll call the whole thing off, and do what he wants you to do, and get a job?' she asked, in her forthright way. It all seemed so simple to Darrell.

Gwen began to sob. 'You don't understand. I couldn't possibly do a thing like that. I'm not going to humble myself. Daddy would crow over me like anything. I'm *glad* I've made him miserable – it'll teach him a lesson!' finished Gwen, so maliciously that Darrell started to her feet.

'You're horrible, Gwen! You don't love your father or anyone else. You only love yourself. You're horrible!'

She went out of the room, and made her way straight to Miss Grayling's room. She had failed utterly and absolutely with Gwen. If Miss Grayling wanted to influence her she must try herself. It was beyond Darrell!

She told Miss Grayling everything. The Head Mistress listened gravely. 'Thank you, Darrell,' she said. 'You did your best, and it was well done. One day Gwen will meet her punishment, and it will, alas, be a terrible one.'

'What do you mean?' said Darrell, half scared by the foreboding tone in Miss Grayling's voice.

'I only mean that when someone does a grievous wrong and glories in it instead of being sorry, then that person must expect a terrible lesson,' said Miss Grayling. 'Somewhere in her life, punishment is awaiting Gwen. I don't know what it is, but inevitably it will come. Thank you, Darrell. You did your best.'

8   The magnet trick

Darrell would not let Gwen and her obstinacy spoil more than a day of her precious last term! She brooded over the interview in her study for a few hours, wishing she could have done better with Gwen – and then put it right out of her mind.

I know I can't do anything more, so what's the good of worrying about it? she thought, sensibly. She turned her thoughts to more interesting things – tennis matches – swimming matches – half-term, when her parents came down – and she also thought about a secret that Felicity had giggled out to her the day before.

'Oh, Darrell. Do listen! Susan's heard of a lovely trick from June. It's *so* simple, and *so* safe.'

Darrell grinned. It was good being high up in school, and an important member of the sixth form – but it did mean that tricks and jokes were no longer possible or permissible. It just wasn't *done* in the sixth, to play a trick on any mistress. The mere thought of playing one on the dignified, scholarly Miss Oakes was impossible.

But there was no reason why the younger ones

shouldn't have their bit of fun, as they had in Darrell's own time. So Darrell grinned and listened, as Felicity poured out her bit of news in a secluded corner of the garden.

'June's getting a magnet,' she said. 'It's a very special one, treated in a special way to make it frightfully powerful. It's very small too, June says – small enough to be hidden in the palm of your hand.'

'Well? What do you intend to do with it?' asked Darrell. There didn't seem to be great possibilities in such an ordinary thing as a magnet.

Felicity began to giggle again. 'Well, you just listen, Darrell,' she said. 'You know how the two Mam'zelles wear their hair, don't you – in little buns?'

Darrell nodded, puzzled. She couldn't for the life of her see what buns of hair and a magnet had to do with each other.

'Mam'zelle Rougier has hers at the back, and Mam'zelle Dupont has hers near the top of her head,' said Felicity. 'And they both stick their buns full of hair-pins.'

Darrell stared at her young sister, and a light began to dawn. 'You don't mean – oh, I say, Felicity – you wouldn't *dare* to hold the magnet near either of the Mam'zelles' heads and make the hair-pins come out!' she said.

Felicity nodded, her eyes dancing. 'Yes. That's the idea,' she said. 'Oh, *Darrell*! Isn't it smashing? It's *super*.'

Darrell began to laugh. 'It's wonderful!' she said. 'Fancy us never thinking of such a simple trick as that. Felicity, when are you going to do it? Oh, I wish I could see it! I wish I could do it myself!'

'You can't. You're head-girl,' said Felicity, sounding quite shocked. 'But you *could* make some excuse, couldn't you, to come and see us play the trick? We thought we'd do it on Mam'zelle Dupont *and* on Mam'zelle Rougier just as many times as they'd stand for it, without getting suspicious.'

'I should think they'd jolly soon get suspicious,' said Darrell. 'Especially Mam'zelle Rougier. You'd better be careful of her, Felicity. She's not got the sense of humour that Mam'zelle Dupont has.'

'We'll be careful,' said Felicity. 'Well – *can* you make an excuse to pop into our classroom, if we tell you when we're going to do the trick?'

'I'll try,' said Darrell. But she felt sure she wouldn't be able to. Mam'zelle might be rather astonished if she kept appearing in the second-form room every time her hair-pins came out!

Darrell told the rest of the form, with the exception of Gwen and Maureen, whom nobody ever trusted enough to let into even the simplest secret. Amanda was there too, and to everyone's surprise, she suddenly guffawed. Like her voice, her laugh was very loud, and it made everyone jump. They hadn't heard the stuck-up Amanda laugh before – she was too busy looking down her nose at everything!

'That's great,' said Amanda. 'We did things like that at Trenigan, too.'

'*Did* you?' said Darrell, in surprise, and Trenigan went a little way up in her rather low estimation of it. 'What tricks did *you* play?'

For the first time Amanda opened out a little, and an animated conversation began about tricks – good ones and bad ones, safe ones and dangerous ones, ones likely to be too easily spotted, and ones that never were spotted. It was a most interesting conversation.

Amanda had to admit that Malory Towers was better at tricks than Trenigan had been.

'Oh well – it's because of Alicia, really, that we got such fine tricks,' said Sally. 'Alicia's got three brothers, and one of them, Sam, always used to send her good tricks he used himself. Alicia – do you remember the sneezing trick?'

'Oh *yes*,' said Alicia. 'It was a tiny pellet, Amanda, which we stuck somewhere near Mam'zelle – on the wall or anywhere, it didn't matter – and when you put a few drops of salt water on it, it sent off an invisible vapour that made people sneeze – and you should have HEARD Mam'zelle sneeze!'

'A-WHOOOOOOOSH-OOO!' said Sally, suddenly, and everyone jumped. Sally grinned. 'Just like that,' she said. 'And poor old Mam'zelle went on and on and on, till she was scared out of her life.'

'Oh dear – how we laughed. I envy those lower-form kids,' said Alicia, putting on a comical look. 'No dignity to keep up, no responsibilities like ours, no necessity to set an example to the whole school. And that wonderful magnet trick to play!'

'Your young cousin June is certainly keeping up the family tradition,' said Mary-Lou. 'When are they going to do this absurd trick?'

It was fixed for a Thursday morning, at the end of the French lesson. This was the last lesson before break and after it the girls would be able to go out into the Court and laugh their heads off, if they needed to!

'Who takes the lesson? Mam'zelle Dupont or Mam'zelle Rougier?' asked Darrell, hoping it was the plump, jolly Mam'zelle Dupont.

But it wasn't. It was the thin, rather bad-tempered Mam'zelle Rougier. What in the world would she think when her hair fell down and her pins disappeared?

The second-formers planned it all carefully. They decided that June must not play the trick. All the teachers were suspicious of her. Somebody else must do the trick.

'Shall I?' said Felicity. 'Or what about Susan? Susan's always so good in class that nobody would ever suspect *her* of such a thing.'

'I'm *not* always good,' said Susan, quite hurt at this compliment. 'Anyway, I don't want to do the trick. I giggle too easily.'

'Nobody must laugh,' warned June. 'Once we laugh we shall be suspected, and we shan't be able to play the trick again.'

'But how can we NOT laugh?' asked Nora, who was given to sudden snorts, like Irene's. 'I mean – laughing is like sneezing or coughing. You can't stop it coming, if it wants to.'

'Yes, you can,' said June, firmly. She had wonderful control over herself, and could keep a straight face during the most comical happenings. 'If you feel you are going to give the game away, you'd better go out of the room just before we do the trick. See?'

'Oh, I *couldn't*. I simply *couldn't* miss it,' said Nora. 'I won't laugh. I'll take three or four hankies and stuff them into my mouth.'

Thursday came. Lessons began. The French lesson came, and Mam'zelle Rougier walked into the room, her heavy tread sounding all the way down the corridor. June was holding open the door. A little snort came from Nora, whose pockets were bulging with handkerchiefs.

'Shut up!' said several people, in loud whispers. Nora looked round, ready to snort again, but met such fierce glares that she subsided.

Mam'zelle Rougier came in. '*Asseyez-vous*,' she said, in her sharp, crisp voice. The class obeyed, sitting down with much scraping of chairs. They looked at Mam'zelle Rougier, suspiciously bright-eyed.

But Mam'zelle Rougier was used to facing dozens of bright, laughing eyes. She snapped out her instructions. 'Page thirty-three. I hope you have prepared the lesson well.' She repeated it slowly in French. 'Nora, please begin.'

Nora was bad at French. She suddenly lost all desire to laugh, and stood up, stammering through the French translation. One by one the others followed. Mam'zelle Rougier was in a bad temper. Words of anger came from her more readily than words of praise that morning! The class felt very pleased she was going to have a trick played on her!

Just before the end of the lesson, Mam'zelle gave her usual order. 'Clean the blackboard, please.'

Susan stood up. She had the powerful little magnet inside the palm of her hand. It had already been tried out on many things, with most miraculous results.

Susan walked steadily to the board near Mam'zelle. Mam'zelle had opened her desk and was rummaging in it for a book. It was a wonderful chance to use the magnet at once!

Watched by twenty-three breathless second-formers,

Susan held the magnet to the back of Mam'zelle's head. She held it about two inches away from the bun of hair on Mam'zelle's neck, as she had been instructed.

Before her delighted eyes, every one of the rather large hair-pins that Mam'zelle Rougier used for her bun flew out, and attached themselves firmly and silently to the magnet. Susan grinned at the class, went abruptly to the blackboard and cleaned it.

Mam'zelle had apparently noticed nothing. The bell went, and she stood up. 'Dismiss!' she said, and the class dismissed, Nora stuffing one of her handkerchiefs into her mouth already. They went to the big hall to get biscuits and milk, watching for Mam'zelle to come too.

She came – and the second-formers gave a squeal of joy. 'It's coming down. The bun's all undone!'

So it was. Mam'zelle hadn't noticed it – but Miss Peters saw it at once. She tapped Mam'zelle on the shoulder and spoke to her. 'Your hair is coming down, Mam'zelle,' she said.

Mam'zelle put up her hand, and to her immense astonishment found that her bun was completely undone and hanging down her back! She groped about for the hair-pins to pin it up again.

There wasn't a single hair-pin in her head! This was not surprising, as they were all on the magnet, which Susan now had safely in her pocket! Mam'zelle Rougier felt frantically all over her head, and Nora gave a muffled snort. She stuffed her second hanky in her mouth.

Mam'zelle now began to feel down her neck, wondering if the hair-pins had disappeared down there. Miss Peters looked at her curiously.

'Lost a hair-pin?' she said.

'I have lost them *all*!' said Mam'zelle, filled with alarm and astonishment. She wondered if she could possibly have forgotten to do her hair that morning. Had she gone into her classes with her hair down her back? She blushed red at the thought. What *must* the girls have thought?

She caught sight of the laughing second-formers, and saw Nora stuffing her third hanky into her mouth. She turned hurriedly and almost ran from the hall.

'The girls were laughing! I *did* come into my classes without pinning up my hair,' said poor Mam'zelle to herself. 'What a thing to do! How could I have forgotten to pin it up? I haven't a single pin in my hair!'

She went to her room and did her hair very carefully indeed. She had no suspicion at all that a trick had been played on her. But if she could have seen the wicked little second-formers laughing and rolling on a secluded piece of grass under the trees in the grounds, she would have felt very suspicious indeed!

'When she groped down her neck for the pins that weren't there!' chuckled June. 'And oh, Miss Peters's face when she saw Mam'zelle's hair all down her back. I could have died.'

'Let's do it again,' begged Felicity. 'Do, do let's. It's one of the funniest tricks we've EVER thought of!'

9 Amanda makes a surprising suggestion

Darrell was working hard for her exam, and so was Sally. But they played hard too, and somehow found time to attend all the debates, the sing-songs, lectures and meetings that cropped up through the week. It was a happy, busy life, and one that Darrell enjoyed to the full.

She had now been six years at Malory Towers and had learned to work really well, so the exam work did not seem as difficult as she expected. Miss Oakes was pleased with her.

'Already you can work by yourself, Darrell, with just a little guidance,' she said. 'You are ready for college now. There, you will find that students can work as much or as little as they like. It is up to them! But you will always work well, and Sally too – you have the habit now.'

Privately Miss Oakes thought that Darrell and Sally would do much better at college than Alicia or Betty, although these two had quicker brains and better memories than either Sally or Darrell.

Being grown-up, and feeling free for the first time from bells and strict time-tables and endless classes, will go to Alicia's head, and Betty's too, thought Miss Oakes. They won't do a scrap of work at college! They'll be out to dances and parties and meetings the whole time – and in the end sound little Darrell and solid little Sally will come away with the honours that Alicia and Betty should find it easy to get – but won't!

At that moment Darrell and Sally were drawing up lists for the first tennis match of the season. Moira was there, giving excellent advice in her rather domineering way. However, Sally put up with that for the sake of her help. Moira knew what she was talking about when it came to games.

Amanda came up and looked silently over their shoulders. The others ignored her. Moira turned her back on her even more pointedly.

'I think for the third team we'll put in Jeanie Smithers, from the third form,' said Sally. 'She's got a very fine serve, and she's steady. She'll make a good couple with Tessie Loman.'

'Tessie's no good,' remarked Amanda. 'Never will be. Not until she gets rid of her peculiar way of serving. She loses half her power, the way she swings her racket.'

'I bet you don't even know which Tessie is!' said Sally.

'Oh yes, I do,' said Amanda, unexpectedly. 'I sometimes go and watch those babies. You can *always* pick out the ones with promise.'

'Well, you're cleverer than we are then,' said Moira. 'It's possible to pick out someone brilliant – and then find it's just a flash in the pan – they're no good at all.'

'I could always pick out the promising ones,' said Amanda, with conviction. 'I could tell you now who to put into the first team – that's easy of course – and the second, third and fourth teams. But I wouldn't choose either Jeanie or Tessie for the third team. They'll go to pieces.'

The others felt annoyed. Why all this interference?

How could Amanda, who had only been a few weeks at Malory Towers, possibly know anything about the sports capabilities of all the girls?

'Well, perhaps you'd like to tell us who will be the captain of school games three years hence?' said Moira, sarcastically. 'We're listening hard!'

'Yes, I can tell you,' said Amanda, without the least hesitation. 'If she had some coaching – proper coaching – and stuck to practising every minute she had, there's a kid in the second form who could be games captain of every form she's in, and far and away best at tennis, whatever form she's in.'

The other three turned and stared at Amanda. She sounded so very very certain.

'Who's the kid?' asked Moira, at last, after all three of them had searched their minds in vain for this elusive second-former. *Who* could it be?

'There you are – you can't even spot her when I've told you she's outstanding, and told you what form she's in,' said Amanda, walking away. 'Why, at Trenigan Towers she would have been spotted the second day she was at school! But you could have a world champion here and never know it!'

'Amanda! Don't go!' ordered Moira. 'Now you've aired your opinions so freely, let's hear a few more. Who's this wonderful second-former?'

'You go and watch them playing, and find out,' said Amanda, in a bored voice. But Moira flew to the door and shut it just as Amanda had opened it to go out. 'No, Amanda,' she said. 'You tell us before you go – or we'll think you're just talking through your hat, and that there isn't any wonderful kid!'

'I don't waste my breath like that,' said Amanda, scornfully. 'And don't glare at me in that way, Moira – you can order the others about as much as you like, and talk to them as if they were bits of dirt – they're used to it! I'm not, and I won't have it. If there's any talk of that sort to be done, *I'll* do it!'

Sally came to Moira's defence, though secretly she was pleased to find someone who could stand up to the opinionated Moira, and fight her on her own level.

'You're a new girl, Amanda,' she said. 'But you seem to forget it. You can't talk to us like that, and you *must* realize that Moira knows more than you do about our girls, even if *I* don't!'

'She doesn't,' said Amanda, contemptuously. 'All right. I'll tell you the kid, and you'll see I'm right. It's June.'

'June!' said the other three, amazed. June, the defiant, aggressive, dare-devil cousin of Alicia's! Well, who would have thought of June?

'She never bothers even to listen when she's being coached,' said Sally.

'She only plays when she wants to,' said Darrell, 'and more often than not she plays the fool! She's no good.'

'June's always been like that,' said Moira. 'Ever since she's been here – she could run faster at lacrosse and tackle better than anyone if she tried – but we have never been able to put her into a team. She could swim like a fish if she didn't always fool about – she's fast when she wants to be. But you can never depend on June.'

'Look,' said Amanda, with conviction in her voice, 'I tell you, if June was coached properly and soundly, at tennis and swimming – I don't know if she's any good at lacrosse, of course – I tell you that kid would be the finest player and swimmer you've ever had. Oh, I know she fools about, I know she's a dare-devil and doesn't care a rap for anyone – but my word, once she finds out she can be superlative at something, well – watch her! She'll go to the top like lightning!'

This was all very surprising – and somehow, spoken in Amanda's loud, very sure voice, it was remarkably convincing. Darrell looked at Sally. Could Amanda be right? Had their dislike and disapproval of the cheeky, don't-care June prevented them from seeing that she had the promise of a first-class games-player?

'Well,' said Sally, doubtfully, thinking of June's tennis, and remembering the way she had watched her playing the fool on the court the week before, 'well, I don't know. She's wonderfully quick and supple, and she's very strong – but her character is against her. She won't *bother.*'

'She just wants someone to take an interest in her and encourage her,' said Amanda. 'I bet it's a case of "give a dog a bad name and hang him", with June. If I had the handling of her, I'd soon make something of her!'

'Well, why don't you?' said Moira, rather dis-agreeably. She had suddenly seen that Amanda was right. June *was* a natural games-player – she had a wonderful eye, and a beautiful style. She's cheeked me so often that I just couldn't see her good points, thought Moira, grimly. She put her question to Amanda, and stood waiting for the answer. 'Well, why don't you?'

'Oh, Amanda can't be bothered to coach *any*one, can you, Amanda?' said Sally, slyly. She felt sure that by appearing doubtful about Amanda's wish to help she would make the big, aggressive girl volunteer to do so. Clever Sally!

Amanda fell into the trap at once. 'I *can* be bothered to coach if the person is worth it,' she said, shortly. 'Well, I'm glad you seem to agree with me, anyway. I'll take on June, and what's more, I'll have her in the second tennis team and second swimming team before the term's finished!'

She walked out, shutting the door loudly, in her usual way. The three left in the room looked at one another. Darrell rubbed her nose as she always did when surprised and taken aback.

'Well! She's right, of course. June *could* be and *would* be a wonder at games if she wanted to. She's like Alicia – brilliant, but unstable. A wonder so long as she's doing something she wants to do, and something she's determined to do well – but no good otherwise.'

'*I* shouldn't care to take that little wretch of a June on,' said Moira. 'She's rude and ungrateful, and she fools about all the time. I wish Amanda joy of her!'

'She's certainly taken on a handful,' said Sally, picking up her games lists. 'But if she *does* help June's game, it'll be something! Anyway, thank goodness we've got Felicity to depend on, Darrell. She's going to follow in your footsteps all right!'

Darrell glowed with pleasure. Yes, Felicity was all right. Felicity would make good – and yet, June would be twice as good as even Felicity, if she only took the trouble!

'Well – it will be interesting to see what happens,' said Moira. 'Very, very interesting. The confident cock-sure Amanda – and the confident cock-sure June. My word, how I do dislike them both!'

10 Amanda and June

When Amanda had made up her mind to do something, she did it immediately. As soon as she had got outside the door she looked out for a second-former, and she saw Susan.

'Hey, you – what's your name – Susan!' she called. 'Go and find June, tell her I want her, and send her up to my study.'

Susan sped off, wondering what June had done. As a rule the second-formers were only sent for when they needed lecturing about something. She found June and delivered the message.

June was surprised. Amanda, as far as she knew, hadn't even bothered to know her name, though she had seen the big sixth-former watching the lower-form tennis practice and swimming several times. She looked at Susan.

'I'm sure it's not me she wants,' she said. 'It's someone else. Anyway, I haven't done anything wrong – and if somebody was going to tick me off, it wouldn't be Amanda. It would be Sally or Darrell. I'm not going. I don't like Amanda.'

'But you *must* go,' said Susan, shocked at the idea of June disobeying a sixth-form order. 'Even if it's a mistake, you ought to go and find out.'

'I'm busy,' said June. 'Leave me alone. I'm the one that will get into trouble for not going, not you. But I shan't, don't worry! Amanda meant someone else, not me.'

Susan went off. All right – let June disobey Amanda if she wanted to. Susan had delivered the message. It was just like June's silly obstinacy. She hated being ordered about by the bigger girls.

Amanda went to her study and waited. She had no real interest in June beyond the fact that she had certainly noted June's decided gift for games. She just wanted to coach her to prove her point. She sat and waited for the second-former to come.

She waited five minutes, patiently, knowing that it might take Susan a little time to find her. Then, most impatiently, she waited another five minutes. She got up, annoyed, and went to the door to see if by any chance June was there and had knocked, and she hadn't heard her.

The passage outside was empty. Amanda went to the window and looked. Down in the garden she saw June, walking with two or three others, talking animatedly. She yelled out of the window.

'June! Come here! Didn't Susan give you my message?'

June pretended not to hear. Amanda yelled again. The others nudged June and pointed to the shouting Amanda. June reluctantly detached herself and went under the window.

'Come up to my study at once,' ordered Amanda. 'I've already been waiting ten minutes and more!'

The other second-formers laughed at June's annoyed face. 'Now you're for it!' called Katherine. 'What have you been up to, June? You're in for a good old wigging!'

June couldn't think of *any*thing she had done. She had hated being hauled indoors in front of all the others. She went in sulkily and stood outside Amanda's door.

She knocked sharply. Amanda had expected a soft, apologetic knock and she jumped.

'Come in,' she said. June went in and shut the door too loudly. She would show Amanda she didn't stand in awe of sixth-formers, however high and mighty they thought themselves!

It was not a good beginning for any co-operation between them. Amanda was annoyed, June was cross.

'I suppose Susan didn't give you my message?' said Amanda.

'Yes, she did,' said June.

'Then why on earth didn't you come?' demanded Amanda.

'I thought you'd made a mistake,' said June. 'I didn't know you even knew my name.'

'What a feeble excuse!' said Amanda and, indeed, it did sound rather feeble, even to June, as she said it.

June scowled. She waited to hear what she had done wrong. She half expected to see a Punishment Book ready on the table, but there was none. All the sixth-formers had Punishment Books, in which they wrote down any punishment they meted out to lower-formers who had offended in some way. Usually the punishment was lines to learn and repeat.

I wish she'd tell me what I've done, thought June, eyeing Amanda aggressively. Actually Amanda, finding June so exasperating, was debating whether or not to change her mind about offering to coach her. She decided to go on with it. She couldn't bear the idea of Moira sneering at her if she didn't.

'Look here, June,' she began, abruptly. 'I've been watching you.'

June was startled. '*Watching* me!' she said, on the defensive at once. 'What for? I'm not aware that I've been worth watching – I've been fairly harmless lately.'

'Don't talk in that silly way,' said Amanda. 'I've been watching you at tennis and swimming. You could be good. In fact you could be better than anyone in the second form *or* the third form. And if you worked at your games, instead of playing the fool, you'd soon beat anyone in the fourth form too.'

June gaped. This was so very extraordinary and unexpected that she couldn't think of a word to say.

Amanda went on.

'So I propose to coach you myself, June. I've told Sally and Darrell and Moira my views about you, and I've said I could make you good enough to put you in the second tennis team and second swimming team before the end of the term. I want to prove that I'm right.'

Still June stared at Amanda, overcome with astonishment. She couldn't understand Amanda picking her out like this. June had no illusions about herself – she knew she could be outstanding if she tried – but it was too much trouble to try! Still, it was very very flattering to be told all this!

'Well?' said Amanda, impatiently. 'Why don't you say something? I propose to begin coaching you right away – this afternoon, if possible.'

June hesitated. She was torn between two alternatives. She disliked Amanda, and wanted to throw her offer back in her face, because it had something hard and condescending about it. On the other hand – what fun to lord it over the other second-formers, and tell them that Amanda, from the great sports school, Trenigan Towers, had actually picked *her* out from all the other lower-formers – and considered it worth while to spend a great deal of time on her!

'All right,' said June, at last. 'Did Sally say I could have special coaching from you?'

Amanda gave a snort. 'Don't be silly. And I think you might at least show a spark of gratitude. I'm going to give up a lot of my time to you.'

'Well – you're really only doing it to prove yourself right, aren't you?' said June, with her devastating sharpness. 'Not because you're really interested in *me*? I don't mind. It suits me, if it suits you!'

Amanda restrained her tongue with an effort. It wouldn't do to put this cheeky youngster in a hostile mood at the beginning, or there would be no co-operation between them, and no good results. But how she did dislike her!

'Very well,' said Amanda, crisply. 'We'll have the whole thing on a business basis. *I* want to prove I'm right, and *you* want to be in the second school teams. At least, I imagine you do. It would be a tremendous thing for a second-former.'

'All right,' said June, in her maddeningly casual way.

'But there's just one thing you must understand,' said Amanda, 'or the whole thing's off. You have jolly well got to come at the times I set for coaching in swimming and tennis. Got that?'

'That's fair enough,' said June. And so the bargain was struck between them, a cold sort of bargain with no liking or real interest on either side. June went off jauntily. What a shock for the other second-formers to hear her news!

As soon as she appeared in the second-form common-room the others called out to her.

'What was it, June? What did she want you for?'

'How many lines have you got to learn *this* time?'

'Did you cheek her? What did you say?'

'She sent for me because she said she wanted to coach me in tennis and swimming,' announced June.

This was so astonishing to the others that they were struck into silence. Felicity gasped.

'Amanda – coaching *you*, June! Whatever for?'

'Well, she appears to think I could be in the second tennis team and the second swimming team by the end of the term if I want to,' said June, airily.

'You couldn't. You always fool about too much,' said Susan at once.

'Right. *Amanda* appears to think so, I said,' answered June. 'I've no doubt your opinion is more correct, though, Susan.'

'Look – don't be so exasperating,' said Felicity. 'Tell us what really happened.'

'I've told you,' said June. 'Amanda wants to coach me every day, and I've agreed. That's all.'

There was another silence. The second-formers found it all very hard to believe. But they knew June was speaking the truth. She always did.

'Well, all I can say is, I wish you joy of being coached by that awful, loud-voiced creature,' said Susan. 'She'll order you about like anything.'

'She'll have to mind her Ps and Qs,' said June, smoothly. 'I don't take kindly to being ordered about. If she wants to prove she's right, and get me good enough for the second teams, she'll have to go about it the right way.'

'You're a pair,' said Harriet. 'A real pair! I shall come and watch the coaching.'

'I don't want you to,' said June, hastily.

'Oh, but we *must*,' said Felicity, winking at the others. 'After all – with coaching marvellous enough to push you into the second teams so soon, even *we* might pick up a few hints.'

'Just a few crumbs from the rich man's table!' giggled Susan. 'Well – what a bit of news!'

11 On the tennis court and in the pool

The news about the special coaching soon flew round the school. The games mistress looked a little doubtful when she heard it. Too much special attention devoted to any one lower-former was not really good.

On the other hand, June *could* be brilliant at games if she was interested enough. Perhaps this offer of Amanda's would really jerk her into working hard at tennis and swimming. If she only worked hard at *some*thing it would be a help to her character!

'She's a maddening child,' Miss Parker, the second-form mistress, remarked to Mam'zelle. 'All that ability of hers for practically everything – and she's just not interested enough to take the trouble to shine. Except at making the others laugh.'

'Yes – she is too good at that,' agreed Mam'zelle, who had suffered from this ability of June's far too often.

'She's superlative at playing the donkey,' said Miss Potts, who had had June in the first form. 'She's about the only child I've ever had in my form that I really would have liked to see the back of!'

They laughed. 'Well, if Amanda can make her keep her nose to the grindstone, it will be very interesting,' said Miss Parker. 'We'll see!'

Amanda drew up a most intensive time-table for June. June gasped when she saw it. A time was set aside every single day for coaching in swimming *and* in tennis. June wondered whether she should protest or not. No – if Amanda was as much in earnest as all that, all right. June would keep her part of the bargain too.

The coaching began. An interested crowd of first and second-formers came to watch. Amanda was astonished to see the crowd, and June didn't like it at all. She didn't want to be laughed at, or barracked all the time.

'What's all this?' said Amanda, waving her hand towards the onlookers sitting round the court on the grass.

'They've come to watch us,' said June. 'They would, of course.'

Amanda addressed the crowd at once.

'If you've come to pick up hints, all right. If not, clear off. Anyone who interrupts the coaching, or disturbs it in any way, can think again. I've got my Punishment Book with me as usual.'

This was greeted by a dead silence, and then, as Amanda turned away, a low and discreet murmur arose. Amanda was decidedly not popular. She was even less popular than the domineering Moira. A few of the girls got up and went away. They had only come to call out funny things to June. Now that it meant their names going down in the Punishment Book, there didn't seem much point in staying. June wished fervently that *every*-one would go. To her great annoyance and surprise she found that she was nervous!

Amanda began with playing pat-ball, keeping a sharp eye on June's returns and placing. She noted that June used her head as well as her hands. She watched the way she swung her racket right back, and kept her eye on the ball. She took in every single detail. There really wasn't much that Amanda didn't know about tennis! She had already played in school-girl championships, and she was a born teacher as well as a born player.

'I say – how long's this going on for?' complained June at last. 'This pat-ball, I mean.'

There was a ripple of laughter from the onlookers. They sat up, hoping that June would begin to be funny.

Amanda didn't answer. She sent another ball over to June. June pretended to miss it, almost fell over and, by a seemingly miraculous recovery, hit the ball from behind her back, and stood up again. This was the kind of clowning she did superlatively well.

There was a wave of laughter from the watchers. 'Go it, June!' called Harriet.

Amanda caught the ball in her hand and swung round to the lower-formers. 'One more shout and off you'll all go,' she announced. 'I can tell you straight away now that there is nothing whatever I can teach June in the way of playing the fool – she knows all the tricks there are – but she doesn't know much about playing real tennis, I'm afraid. Do you see how badly she plays a backhand ball? She goes like this – instead of like this! And did you notice her feet when she played those balls off the right-hand side? All wrong!'

June stood still, fuming. Why point out her faults to the audience? But she knew why, of course. It was Amanda's return for that bit of clowning. Every time she clowned, and a laugh came, Amanda would stop and point out other faults of June's!

The next time a ball went near where the spectators were, June spoke to them in a low voice.

'I wish you'd clear off. It's jolly difficult trying to concentrate with you all looking.'

But they didn't clear off, especially when Amanda stopped the pat-ball play and began to explain to June, in her loud, dominating voice, the few hundred things she did wrong. It was wonderful to see the don't-care June having to stand there like someone from the kindergarten and listen to all her tennis failings! The lower forms really enjoyed it.

June didn't enjoy it at all. If she had been a weaker character she would have made up her mind to call the whole thing off, and refuse to be coached again. But June was not weak – and besides, she couldn't help realizing that Amanda really did know what she was talking about. And Amanda also knew how to be patient and how to explain a thing simply and clearly.

June found herself looking at Amanda with unwilling admiration as she illustrated, by various swings of her racket and placing of her feet, exactly what she meant.

I've learned more in this one coaching than I've learned in a whole term, thought June. But she didn't tell Amanda that. She wasn't going to hand the loud-voiced Amanda any bouquets!

Amanda didn't hand June any bouquets either. She merely said, 'That's enough for today. You've plenty of things to think about, as you can see. Get some of them right for next time. And be down at the swimming-pool to the minute tomorrow morning. I've only ten minutes to give you, and I don't want a second wasted.'

June *was* down to the minute. Amanda was there exactly on time too. She put June through a very gruelling ten minutes, and found as many faults with her swimming as she had done with her tennis. Darrell, Moira and Mary-Lou happened to be there too, and they watched in silence.

'If June can stick it, this is going to do her a world of good,' said Darrell. 'My word – what a driver Amanda is – she never lets up for a moment.'

'June *can* stick it all right. The question is – will she?' said Mary-Lou. 'I have a feeling she'll get very tired of all this soon – not the coaching, but the way it's done. So ruthless, somehow.'

Three or four second-formers came down to swim, among them Josephine, fat and pasty-looking, airing her opinions as usual. They weren't worth anything of course. They never were. But, like her father, she loved hearing the sound of her voice, and if she could boast about anything, she did.

She had plenty to boast about. 'My father has a whole *fleet* of cars! My mother has a diamond necklace she

73

never wears because it's too valuable. We've a dog at home worth five hundred pounds. My aunt's sending me five pounds for my birthday. My brother's got . . .'

These were the items of family news that Jo continually talked of. There was no doubt at all that they were true.

'Miss Parker is an old nosey! I meant to get out of swimming this morning, and of course she must come and poke her nose in and send me out. I told her what I thought of her. I said . . .'

'Shut up,' said Amanda, who was shouting instructions to June in the water. 'Shut up, and get into the water. I'm coaching someone.'

Jo gave a giggle. She hadn't at first recognized Amanda in her swimming-costume. 'Oh, it's Amanda. Oh, do let's watch this. It'll be as good as the tennis.'

She happened to get in Amanda's way, and impatiently Amanda gave her a push. Into the water went Jo with an agonized squeal. The others yelled with laughter.

But Jo had gone into a deep part, and she couldn't swim. She came up, gasping and terrified, trying to feel the bottom with her feet. But there was no bottom to feel. She went under again.

'Look – quick – Jo's in the deep water!' yelled Darrell. 'She can't swim.'

June swam up to the struggling Jo, and began to life-save her. But Jo was now completely out of control, and so terrified that she clutched hold of June and dragged her under too. She was fat and heavy, and June could do nothing with her.

There was a splash as Amanda dived neatly in. In a moment she was by Jo and had gripped her. 'Let go, June!' she ordered. 'I'll manage her!'

Jo clutched blindly at Amanda, who saw there was only one thing to be done. She must bring Jo back to her senses immediately – and she could only do that by giving her a sharp shock. Otherwise it would take ages to get the terrified girl to the edge of the pool.

She raised her hand and slapped Jo very sharply on the right cheek. The slap echoed round the pool. Jo gasped and came to her senses at once, very angry indeed.

'That's right. Now you listen to me,' ordered Amanda, sharply. 'Don't clutch. I've got you all right. Lie still and I'll take you to the edge.'

It was only a few seconds before Amanda had got Jo to the edge, and Moira and Darrell and Mary-Lou were hauling her up.

Jo collapsed. She wailed. She howled. 'I nearly drowned. You hit me! I'll write to my father and tell him you pushed me in, you big bully!' she wailed. 'I feel awful. I nearly drowned. Oh, my cheek does hurt where you slapped me!'

'Don't be silly,' said Moira. 'You didn't nearly drown. You just lost control of yourself. You didn't even *try* to swim though you've been having lessons!'

'Amanda got you out all right,' said Mary-Lou, gently, seeing that Jo had been really frightened. 'She didn't know you couldn't swim or she wouldn't have pushed you in.'

'She's a bully,' wept Jo. 'I'll tell my father.'

'Tell him,' said Amanda. 'The only thing that's wrong with you is that you're a little coward. I'll give *you* special coaching too, if you like – I'll have you swimming like a fish in a couple of lessons!'

That was the last thing Jo wanted. She dressed and, still weeping and uttering threats, went back to the school. The others laughed.

'Poor Jo! She doesn't fit in at Malory Towers,' said Mary-Lou. 'What a little idiot she is!'

12 The days go by

Jo got very little sympathy from anyone except a small first-former called Deirdre. Deirdre met her as she was coming up from the pool, still weeping.

'Oh! What's the matter, Jo?' asked Deirdre, in distress. 'Have you hurt yourself?'

'I've been practically *drowned*,' said Jo, more tears springing out. 'That brute of an Amanda pushed me into the deep end, though she *knew* I couldn't swim. She slapped me too – look! I shall tell my father.'

'Oh, I should,' said Deirdre, flattered at the way this second-former was talking to her, a first-former. Deirdre couldn't swim either, and she could quite well understand what fear Jo had felt when she had been pushed into the deep end of the pool. 'How wicked of Amanda. Nobody likes her and I'm not surprised.'

Jo sat down on a ledge of rock, halfway up the cliff. She wiped her eyes with her hand. 'I don't feel well,' she said. 'I feel beastly. I'm sure I'm chock-full of sea water. I shan't be able to eat anything at all today.'

This seemed dreadful to Jo, and almost as dreadful to Deirdre, who had a very good appetite. She ventured to feel Jo's arm.

'You're shivering,' she said. 'You'd better go in. Shall I fetch Matron for you?'

'Oh goodness, no,' said Jo, at once. She had no more love for Matron than Matron had for Jo. Matron had too often seen through Jo's pretences and evasions. One of them was a bad headache on the afternoons when a long walk was prescribed!

'Funny,' Matron had said. 'Long walk – headache. The two always go together with you, Jo. Well, you can take your headache on the long walk. It'll do it good!'

So Jo certainly didn't want any attention from Matron on the morning when she had been 'practically drowned'. All Jo wanted was sympathy and a lot of it.

But the only sympathy she got was from the little first-former, Deirdre. Everyone else laughed at her.

'Practically *drowned*!' said Susan, scoffing. 'You just went under and got a mouthful of water, Jo.'

'I'll hold you under for a lot longer if you *really* would like to know what being "practically drowned" is like,' offered June, when she had heard Jo's laments about six times.

'Jo's been practically drowned at least twelve times,' said Dawn. 'I can't think why she doesn't *try* and learn to swim. Then she wouldn't keep on getting "practically drowned"!'

'I don't know why you're so mean to me,' said Jo, looking pathetic. 'Don't I share my sweets and cakes and everything with you? Didn't I tell you I'd just got twenty-five pounds from my aunt to spend on a birthday feast?

You know we'll have a jolly good time on my money. Don't I always . . .'

'Be quiet,' said Felicity, crossly. 'Don't we *all* share our things with one another? You're not the only one!'

'Yes, but I get so many *more* things,' said Jo. 'Look at that enormous cake I had last week – it lasted our table two days. And look at . . .'

'Don't keep on pushing your riches down our throats!' said June, exasperated. 'And keep your cakes and sweets to yourself in future. I don't want any. You keep on and on reminding us of them. Eat them all yourself!'

Jo's eyes filled with tears. 'You're mean,' she said. 'You're all horrid. One of these days I'll run away!'

'Do,' said June. 'It would be too wonderful for words to wake up one morning and find your bed empty. What a relief!'

Jo sniffed dolefully and went in search of Deirdre again. She knew Deirdre would be sympathetic. And so she was – especially when Jo produced a big box of chocolates that had come the day before, and which, so far, she hadn't shared with anyone.

'I shan't give the second-formers one single chocolate,' Jo declared. 'We'll have them all, Deirdre. Go on – take half the box back with you. And when my next cake comes I'll give you a quarter of it!'

Deirdre had no mother to send her any cakes or sweets. She had only a father, who was at sea, and an old aunt who didn't realize that little girls liked parcels at boarding school. So she was very thrilled with the chocolates indeed. They were magnificent ones too, as Jo's always were.

'My family never get anything but the best,' Jo said.

She found that she could boast as much as she liked to Deirdre, who drank it all in. 'I wish you could see my bedroom at home, Deirdre – it's all red and gold – and I've got a little bathroom of my own too, done in red and gold.'

This was perfectly true. Jo's father was rolling in money. Jo once boasted that there wasn't anything her father couldn't buy. June had inquired whether he had enough money to buy himself a few hundred Hs. Jo had never forgiven June for that. For the first time she had realized that her father's loud-voiced remarks were made all the worse by the way he continually dropped his Hs, and by his curious lapses in grammar.

Amanda actually came after Jo one morning to ask her if she *would* like her to coach her in swimming. She had felt rather guilty about pushing Jo in, and had kicked herself for not finding out first if she could swim. Jo turned her back rudely on Amanda.

'No thanks,' she said curtly. 'It's a good thing for you I *didn't* write and tell my father. Anyway I wouldn't be put through what you're giving June for anything in the world. No *thank* you!'

Sally was with Amanda. She swung Jo round by the shoulder. 'Now just apologize to Amanda for your rudeness,' she said. 'Go on, quick!'

'No,' said Jo, seeing the admiring Deirdre nearby.

'Very well,' said Sally, whipping out her little Punishment Book. 'You can learn any piece of poetry in your French poetry book, so long as it's not shorter than twenty lines. And say it to me before Wednesday next.'

'I apologize,' said Jo, sulkily. French was not one of her best subjects.

'Too late,' said Sally. 'The punishment stands. And take that scowl off your face.'

'No. Hold it!' said Belinda's voice from the back, and out came her sketch book. 'It isn't often I get such a nice fine *fat* scowl! Aha – see yourself, young Jo!'

Jo gazed in anger at the caricature of herself – wickedly like her at her most bad-tempered. She turned on her heel and slouched off, Deirdre following her like a faithful little dog.

'That kid wants taking in hand,' said Sally. 'I hear from Felicity that she gets parcels practically every day from home – really extravagant ones too. And the money she gets! If I catch her flinging it about I shall confiscate it or send her to Matron. Those lower-formers have got to stick to the rules where money is concerned. It isn't fair to the others, who only have a couple of pounds a term to spend. She's a pest, that kid.'

The interest in Amanda's coaching of June soon died down. June stuck it, though sometimes with a bad grace. Amanda never praised – that was the worst of her. She found fault dozens of times, but even when June really did produce an ace of a serve, Amanda's only comment would be, 'Well, it's pleasant to see a good serve at last!'

Amanda herself soon proved to everyone that she was far and away the best in the school at tennis and swimming. She was put automatically into the first team for swimming and diving and the first tennis team too. It was a joy to watch her swim or play. Darrell never ceased to marvel at the grace of her great hefty body on the tennis court or in the pool.

Moira and Amanda had many squabbles, especially over helping the younger ones. Moira was very good about this, but Amanda took no interest at all.

'Tessie's got to learn how to place her balls better,' she would say. Or, 'Lucy would be better if she stopped yelling about at swimming and practised a bit more. She'd be good then.'

'Well – what about telling Tessie, and showing Lucy what she should do?' Moira would say, impatiently. 'You always see what's wrong – but you never never want to put it right. Except for June. She's the only one.'

Amanda didn't answer. She didn't seem to be listening and this always annoyed Moira more than anything.

'That's right. Look away in the distance and think of the wonderful days when you'll win everything at the Olympic Games,' sneered Moira, going out of the room.

Moira would have liked to be as good as Amanda was at games. They were her greatest interest, much to the French girl, Suzanne's, perpetual astonishment.

'This Moira, this Amanda,' she said to Mam'zelle Dupont. '*Elles sont très drôles*!'

'Speak in English, Suzanne,' Mam'zelle would say, severely. 'How many times must I tell you this?'

'Police?' said Suzanne.

'You heard me,' said Mam'zelle. 'Now – say what you said – in English, please.'

'This Moira, this Amanda – they – are vairy piggy-hoo-learrr!' said Suzanne, earnestly.

Mam'zelle stared at her. '*What* was that word?' she asked, astonished.

'Piggy-hoo-learrrrr!' repeated Suzanne. 'It is a true word, Mam'zelle Dupont. Darrell tiched it me.'

'Darrell taught you?' said Mam'zelle. 'Ah, I must ask her what it is.'

It turned out to be 'peculiar', of course, and for some time after that everything odd was referred to as 'piggy-hoo-learrrrr'! Alicia took it upon herself to teach Suzanne a few more words, which also astonished poor Mam'zelle very much.

She taught the unsuspecting Suzanne such words as 'fiddlesticks!', 'piffle', and 'scrumplicious', which, of course, was a mixture of scrumptious and delicious.

Suzanne liked the words very much, and used them whenever she could. She described Mam'zelle's new lace collar as 'scrumpleeeecious!' and amiably told her that in her opinion swimming was 'peefle' and 'vairy feedle-steecks' and didn't Mam'zelle agree with her?

'What is this "peefle" and "feedlesteecks"?' Mam'zelle asked suspiciously. 'They are not words. Alicia, have you ever heard of them, tell me truly?'

'Oh yes, Mam'zelle,' said Alicia, gazing innocently at Mam'zelle. She caught sight of a hair-pin coming out of Mam'zelle's bun, and the sight made her remember the wonderful magnet. Had June used it again? She must find out.

'Peefle,' muttered Mam'zelle, feverishly searching through the dictionary for it. 'Peefle. He is not here, this peefle. Suzanne, take this dictionary and look through it carefully for me.'

'Police?' said Suzanne, politely. Mam'zelle exploded.

'Yes – look up your everlasting "police", too!' she cried. 'See what it means. One day they will be after you – the POLICE! Ah, you foolish girl. Never will you learn to spik the English as he should be spoke.'

13 A shock – and a nice little plot

Alicia remembered to ask June about the magnet. June grinned at her, put her hand into the pocket of her navy-blue gym skirt and pulled out the neat, powerful little magnet.

Alicia took it. It was very heavy. She slid it along the desk. A large pencil-sharpener appeared almost to leap through the air and fasten itself on the magnet. Then a compass came, and two or three paper-clips.

'We played the trick on Mam'zelle Rougier again,' said June. 'Harriet did it that time. We did it a bit differently, and it was just as funny.'

'What happened?' asked Alicia.

'Well, the hair-pins came out again, of course,' said June, smiling broadly. 'And Harriet quickly took them off the magnet, and dropped them by the door when she went back to her place. Mam'zelle Rougier felt her hair going down her back and put up her hand to see, of course. She couldn't find a single pin and looked absolutely horrified.

'Then Felicity put up her hand and said she had seen some hair-pins down by the door, and were they Mam'zelle's by any chance?

'Mam'zelle simply couldn't understand how they had got there. We offered all kinds of explanation. I said Mam'zelle must have dropped them coming in. Harriet said she didn't think they could be Mam'zelle's, and how lucky it was that somebody else had dropped hair-pins in our classroom, and . . .'

'Mam'zelle Rougier will be smelling rats if you offer too many explanations,' said Alicia, with a laugh.

'I think she does smell a rat, actually,' said June. 'She keeps on and on putting up her hand to her hair to see if it's still up, and she fingers her hair-pins all day long to make sure they're still there! And she looks frightfully suspiciously at us now!'

'I wish I could see it played on Mam'zelle Dupont,' sighed Alicia. 'She's the one that would be the funniest.'

'Yes. It's a pity sixth-formers are too high and mighty to play a little joke,' said June. 'I hope I'm not like that if ever I get into the sixth.'

'You won't be much good if you aren't,' said Alicia. 'Well – it's a good trick. I'd like to have had it when *I* was in the second form. I think I'd have used it to more effect than you appear to have, though!'

She went off. June looked after her. Now how would Alicia have used it to better effect? It couldn't be done! June put the magnet back slowly into her pocket, her quick mind going over all that Alicia had said.

She sought out Felicity and Sally, and the three of them put their heads together. Jo came into the room and saw them. She went over, all agog at once.

'What's the secret? What's up?' she said.

'Nothing,' said June.

'You *might* tell me,' said Jo, offended. 'I do think you're mean. I'm always kept out of everything. *I* always share things. I'm planning to have a first-class feast next week. Look – I've got twenty-five pounds!'

For about the fourth time that day she took the notes

out of the pocket of her tunic to show the others. She did not dare to keep them in her drawer in case Matron found them and removed them.

'We've seen them too many times already,' said Felicity, bored. 'What's your father going to send you for your birthday? A Rolls Royce? Or a string of race-horses? Or will he be too mean for words and only send you a real pearl necklace?'

Jo turned away angrily. How was it she never never could learn not to show off? Felicity wondered. Did she take after her parents so closely that she had all their mannerisms and habits too?

A most unfortunate thing happened to Jo just after she had left the common-room. The pocket of her tunic wore through – and it happened to be the one in which she kept her money! No doubt much pulling in and out of notes had weakened it. Anyway, it quietly frayed, and Jo didn't know it.

She wandered down the corridor, feeling the familiar sensation of being left out in the cold. What had those three been mumbling about? *Why* didn't they tell her? She determined to go and find Deirdre and talk against the second-formers once more. Deirdre was always a willing listener, and a more than willing sharer of Jo's many goodies.

Matron came out of her room just as Jo had passed. She was most astonished to see a five-pound note lying on the floor. She picked it up. It had fallen out of Jo's pocket, of course, and Jo hadn't noticed it. Matron stuffed it into her pocket and went on again. She came across a second five-pound note, lying in the middle of the corridor. How very extraordinary!

Matron became suspicious. Were they real notes – or was this somebody's joke? Were there bright eyes watching her pick them up? Matron glanced round, but there was no one to be seen at all. She looked at the notes. They certainly seemed genuine enough.

She was really amazed when she came across the third one. It was just round the corner, and lay there, flapping a little in the draught of the corridor. Matron picked it up thoughtfully. Surely they couldn't belong to any of the girls? Nobody had so much at once!

'Fifteen pounds,' she said to herself. 'Fifteen pounds – and not given in to me! And HOW did they come to be here, lying around like this?'

The last two notes lay together in a corner of the corridor near the garden door. Matron pounced on them. 'Twenty-five now! Well, well, well – somebody very rich has been walking along here – but why cast away so much money?'

Matron looked out of the door. She saw two figures in the distance – Deirdre and Jo, talking together earnestly.

A light dawned on Matron. Of course! Jo! Some of her wealthy relations had been providing her with illicit pocket-money again. But twenty-five *pounds*! How foolish Jo's people were. They were ruining her with their silly, extravagant ideas!

Jo must have dropped them. Matron stood by the door and frowned. Had Jo any more money than this? She should, of course, have given it in to Matron – that was the strict rule. She saw Jo pull at her tunic and slip her hand into her pocket. Ah – so that was where the money was kept!

And then, of course, Jo found the hole – and no

notes! She gave a cry of horror and alarm.

Matron disappeared. She went back to her room. She put the money into her safe and wrote out a notice in her firm, clear handwriting.

Meantime Jo looked at Deirdre in horror when she discovered her money was gone. 'Look – there's a hole in my pocket! I must have dropped the notes. Come on, quickly – we must look for them! They can't be far away.'

But, of course, the money was gone. Not a penny could poor Jo find. She wept in dismay, and Deirdre tried to comfort her.

Jo met June, Felicity and Susan coming down the corridor, looking very pleased with themselves. They had made a very nice little plan, with the magnet as the centre of it! Jo rushed up to them.

'I've lost my money – all of it! Do you know if anyone's found it?'

'There'll soon be a notice put up on the big board, if anyone has,' said Felicity, and the three went on, not at all inclined to let Jo weep on their necks.

'Beasts! Unkind beasts!' said Jo. 'Why did I ever come here? Deirdre, you're the only decent person in the school – the only one I can depend on. I've a good mind to run away!'

Deirdre had heard this many times before. 'Oh no,' she said comfortingly. 'You mustn't do that, Jo dear. Don't say things like that!'

Felicity and the others laughed to see Jo on her knees in the corridor, still searching for the notes, when they came back. They had already seen Matron's notice on the big board. What a shock for Jo when she knew who had found her money!

'Look on the notice-board,' said June. 'Someone has found your money, Jo, you'll be glad to know. You can get it back in two minutes!'

Thankfully Jo got to her feet and rushed off with Deirdre to read the notice. June laughed. 'I wonder what Matron will say to Jo,' she said. 'That is – if Jo dares to go and ask for the money!'

But Jo didn't interest them for more than a minute. They were too pleased with their plot to forget it for long. They had been looking for Nora to tell it to. Nora would be sure to laugh her head off!

They found her at last. 'Listen, Nora,' said June. 'You know my cousin Alicia? Well, she saw our magnet today and she said if *she* had had it she would have played a much better trick than we did – and she was moaning and groaning because she's in the sixth and they're too priggish to play tricks any more.'

'So we decided we'd give the sixth form a treat,' broke in Felicity. 'And one of us is going to appear in their room with a message to Mam'zelle Dupont, when she's taking a lesson there – and extract all her pins, and then go!'

'And Mam'zelle will think one of *them* has been up to something,' said Susan. 'They simply won't know what to do!'

'We thought we might do it twice or three times, just to show the sixth we play our tricks as well as they could,' said June.

Nora went off into squeals of laughter. 'Oh, let me be the one to go,' she begged. 'Do, do, do! I swear I won't giggle. It's only when I'm with the second form I keep wanting to laugh, and can't stop. I'll be as solemn as a judge if you'll let me go.'

'Well, we thought we *would* choose you,' said June. 'Mam'zelle might suspect *us* – we've played tricks on her before – but she'd never suspect you – you're one of her favourites too, so she'll be quite pleased to see you.'

Nora was the fluffy-haired big-eyed type that Mam'zelle always loved. She twinkled at the three plotters. 'I'll do it!' she said, with a chuckle. 'I'll do it three times if you want me to!'

'Oh no – somebody else must do it next,' said June. 'We don't want Mam'zelle to get suspicious – and she would if you kept on appearing!'

'Especially if her hair fell down each time,' giggled Susan. 'Golly, I wish I was going to be there!'

'Here comes Jo!' whispered June. 'My word, she looks petrified!'

Jo *was* petrified! She had gone to the notice-board and had seen Matron's notice at once.

Will the person who dropped twenty-five pounds in five-pound notes along the corridor please come to me?

MATRON

Jo could have dropped through the floor. *Matron*! Now whatever was she to do? If there was one person poor Jo really dreaded, it was Matron!

14 Problems for Amanda

Poor Jo lamented loud and long to Deirdre about her bad luck. To think that *Matron* had the money! How in the world could she explain to Matron that she had had twenty-five pounds – *twenty-five pounds* – and not handed it in for safe custody as usual?

'Jo, you'll just have to go and tell her,' said Deirdre, anxiously. 'If you don't, you might not get the money back, ever. If Matron doesn't know who it belongs to, how *can* she give it back?'

'Well, I suppose I'd better,' said Jo. But she had no sooner got to the door than she came back. 'I can't,' she said to Deirdre. 'I daren't face her. Don't think me a coward, Deirdre, but honestly I shake at the knees when Matron puts on that face of hers and says the most awful things.'

Timid little Deirdre had never had any awful things said to her by Matron, but she knew she would feel the same as Jo if she had. She stared at Jo. How were they to get out of the difficulty?

'Jo – I suppose you couldn't slip into Matron's room when she's not there, and just see if the money is lying anywhere about, could you?' she said, in a half whisper. 'After all – it's yours. You would only be taking what belongs to you!'

Jo's little eyes gleamed. 'Yes!' she said. 'I might be able to do that – if only Matron *has* got the money somewhere loose. I know I've seen some tied up in neat packages on her table sometimes – petty cash, I suppose. She might have put mine there, too, ready to hand out to the loser.'

'She wouldn't hand it out,' said Deirdre. 'You know that. She'd keep it and dole it out. All the lower-formers have their pocket-money doled out to them. You'd probably get just a bit of it each week, and the rest would be handed back to you when you go home for the holidays.'

Jo frowned. 'I meant to spend that money on a terrific feast,' she said. 'It's my birthday soon, you know. I simply *must* get it somehow.'

'Sh,' said Deirdre. 'Someone's coming.'

It was Felicity. She poked her nose round the door and grinned. 'Got your money back yet, Jo?' she said. 'Or are you going to make a present of it to Matron? I know *I* wouldn't care to go and own up to having twenty-five pounds – especially if I had been careless enough to lose it too! What an ass you are.'

'Shut up, Felicity,' said Jo. 'I've had enough of people getting at me all the time. I can't think why you're all on to me every minute of the day. Anyone would think I wasn't fit to be at Malory Towers.'

As this was exactly what most of the second-formers did think, Felicity made no reply. Jo never would fit, she was certain. If she had had parents who would have backed up the school, and helped Jo, there might have been a chance for her.

But they laugh at the rules of the school, they tell Jo not to bother to keep any rule if she doesn't want to, they send her parcels of things she's not supposed to have, and far too much money, thought Felicity, going off to practise serving at tennis. Her father keeps saying she's only to enjoy herself, and not to bother to work hard – *he* was always at the bottom of the form, and yet now he's rolling in money – so he thinks it doesn't matter if Jo's at the bottom too!

It was puzzling that some parents backed up their children properly, and some didn't. Surely if you loved your children you *did* try to bring them up to be decent in every way? And yet Jo's father *seemed* to love her. It puzzled Felicity. If he really did love her, how could he encourage her to break rules, to be lazy, to do all the wrong things? How could he laugh when he read disapproving remarks on Jo's reports?

Jo said he clapped her on the back and roared with laughter when he read what Miss Parker had written at the bottom of her report last term, remembered Felicity. What was it she wrote, now? 'Jo has not yet learned the first lesson of all – the difference between plain right and wrong. She will not get very far until she faces up to this lesson.' Gosh – if I'd had that on my report, Daddy would have been broken-hearted, and I should have got the most awful rowing. But Jo's father only laughed!

Felicity found Susan, who was going to take her practice serves. Soon they were on a court, and Felicity was lamming the balls hard at the patient Susan. Amanda wandered up after a time and watched. Felicity redoubled her efforts at serving well.

Since Amanda had taken on June and was training her so well, every lower-former hoped to be singled out for a little attention from the big sixth-former. Felicity sent

down one or two fast serves, and Susan called out to Amanda.

'She's good, isn't she, Amanda?'

'So-so,' said Amanda, and turned away, not appearing in the least interested.

'Beast!' said Susan, under her breath. 'Moira would at least have said yes or no – and if Felicity was doing something wrong she'd have set her right, and if she was doing well, she would have praised her.'

Actually Amanda had hardly noticed Felicity's play. She was thinking hard about something. About two things, in fact. She was worried about June – not about her progress, which was, in fact, amazing. Amanda knew how and what to teach, and June was a very able and quick pupil – but June was getting tired of Amanda's strictness and lack of all praise. She was becoming annoyed with the sharp commands and curt orders. It had never been easy for June to knuckle under to anyone, and to be ordered about by someone she really disliked was getting a little too much for her.

She had said so to Amanda the day before. Amanda had taught her a fast new swimming-stroke, and had insisted on her thrashing her way up and down the pool, up and down. Then she had gone for June because she hadn't paid attention to some of her shouted instructions.

'You deliberately swam all the way up the pool using your legs wrong,' she said. 'I yelled at you, but you went on and on.'

'Do you suppose I can hear a word when water is in my ears, and my arms are thrashing over my head like thunder?' demanded the panting June. 'It's true that even the school could probably hear your voice, and no doubt

95

they could even hear it at the post office, a mile away – it's always loud enough! But I *couldn't*, so you'd better get a megaphone. Though I grant you your voice is better than *any* megaphone, at any time, in any place. Why, even at church . . .'

'That's enough,' said Amanda, angrily. 'I don't take cheek from a second-former.'

'And I'm beginning to feel I won't take orders from a sixth-former,' said June, drying herself with a towel. 'I've had almost enough. So I warn you, Amanda.'

Amanda was about to say something really cutting, but stopped herself. She had begun to be very proud of June. June was a most marvellous pupil, although unfriendly and usually silent. It would be a pity to stop the coaching now that June was almost as perfect as she could hope to be at tennis and swimming. She was quite good enough for the second team now, and Amanda meant to ask to have her tried out for it in a week or two's time.

So Amanda turned away, fuming inwardly, but trying not to show it. June grinned to herself. She knew quite well that Amanda didn't want to give up the coaching now that June was proving her right in what she had said to the others. All the same, thought June, I'm getting tired of it. This is a most unpleasant term, slaving like this. Do I really, honestly, care enough about being in the second team to go through all this? I'm not sure that I do!

That was June all over, of course. If she took enough trouble, and cared enough, she could shine at anything. But there seemed to be a flaw in her strong character that caused her not to care enough about things.

June was one of the problems that occupied Amanda's mind. The other was her own swimming. Swimming was perhaps her most magnificent achievement in the sports line. To see Amanda hurtle across the pool was a sight in itself. Nobody could swim even one half as fast. Even the small first-formers stopped their chattering when Amanda took to the water.

And what Amanda was thinking hard about was her swimming. The pool wasn't enough for her. She wanted to swim right out to sea. How could she get enough practice for really long-distance swimming if she didn't swim in the sea? The pool was wonderful – wide and long and deep – but after all, it was only a pool. Amanda wanted to swim for at least a mile! Two miles, she thought, exultantly, three miles! I am strong enough to swim the Channel, I really do believe.

At Trenigan, where her old school had been, the sea coast was safer than the treacherous Cornish coast at Malory Towers, with its strong currents, and vicious rocks on which great waves pounded day and night. But Amanda was sure she could overcome even a strong current.

No one was allowed to swim right out to sea at Malory Towers. That was an unbreakable rule. Anyone wanting real sea-swimming from the shore could go in a party to another beach some way along, and swim in safety from there. But no one was allowed to swim out from the shore at Malory Towers.

No one even wanted to! Enormous waves ran up the rocks to the pool. Even on a calm day, the blue water surged and heaved, and swept with great force over the rocks. Amanda, who loved the strength of water, longed to battle with the fierce sea here. She was quite fearless in all physical things.

She had hardly seen Felicity's tennis, as she stood by the court, idly following the ball with her eyes. Should she take a chance, and go swimming out to sea some time? She didn't much care if she got into a row or not. She wasn't going to stay very long at Malory Towers, and the rules didn't frighten *her*! She suddenly made up her mind.

I *will* go swimming out to sea, she decided. I've talked to Jack the fisherman, and he's told me what currents there are. If I went down to the edge of the rocks at low tide, I could dive off into deep water, and avoid the worst currents by swimming to the west, and then straight out. I should be all right.

The thing was – when could she do this unnoticed? Not that she *minded* getting into a row – but it was silly to do that if it could be avoided. Amanda turned the matter over in her mind.

Early morning would be best, she thought. *Very* early morning. Nobody would be about then. I could have about an hour and a half's real swimming. It would be heaven!

Having settled that, Amanda felt happy. She wished she could settle the June business as easily. But that didn't altogether rest with her! She wasn't going to give in to June's ideas as to how she should be coached, and if June chose to be rude and make things difficult, then there might be a serious row.

'I don't *want* one!' said Amanda to herself. 'But if June provokes one, perhaps it will clear the air, and let her know where she stands. I'm certainly not going to put up with any nonsense, and I think if it came to the point, June wouldn't be idiot enough to throw away her chance of being put in the second school teams.'

15 Half-term

Half-term came and went. It was brilliant weather and the parents thoroughly enjoyed themselves wandering over the school grounds and down by the sea.

The enclosed garden, set in the hollow square in the middle of the four-towered building, was very popular. It was crammed with hundreds upon hundreds of rose-bushes, and the sight and scent of these filled the fathers and mothers with delight.

'I'm glad Malory Towers is at its very best my last half-term,' Darrell said to her mother, as she took her to see the roses. 'I shall always remember it like this. Oh, Mother, thank you a thousand times for choosing this school for me. I've been so happy here.'

Her mother squeezed her arm. 'You've done very well indeed at Malory Towers,' she said. 'All the mistresses have been telling me how much they will miss you, and what a help you've always been. They are glad you have a sister to follow in your footsteps!'

Gwen went by with her mother and Miss Winter. 'My last half-term!' she was saying. 'Fancy, my next half-term will be in *Switzerland*. I'm sure I shall be much happier there than I've ever been here.'

Gwen's father had not come. Gwen was glad. 'I was afraid he might come and spoil everything,' she said to her mother. 'He was so horrid to us last holidays, wasn't he?'

'He would have come,' said Miss Winter. 'But he's not well. He hasn't really been well for some time, Gwen. You should have written to him this term, you know. I really do think you should.'

'It's not your business,' said Gwen, coldly. 'Honestly, you can't always tell whether Daddy isn't well, or is just bad-tempered, can you, Mother? Anyway, we shan't miss him today.'

'Where's Maureen?' asked Mrs. Lacy. Maureen, so like Gwen, with her fluffy golden hair and big, pale-blue eyes, was quite a favourite with Mrs. Lacy and the old governess. But Gwen wasn't going to have anything to do with Maureen that day! Maureen 'sucked up' to Gwen's people and they just loved it.

'Maureen's got her own people here today,' she said. 'Poor Maureen – I'm sorry for her, Mother. *She's* not going to a finishing school, or even to college of any sort. She's just going to take a secretarial course, and go into somebody's office!'

Jo's people came by, with Jo hanging on to her father's arm. The big, loud-voiced, vulgar man could, as usual, be heard all over the place.

'Not a bad little rose-garden this, Jo, eh?' he said. 'Course it's not a patch on ours. Let's see, Ma, how many roses have we got in our rose-garden?'

'Five thousand,' said Mrs. Jones, in a low voice. She was always rather overawed by the other parents, and she was beginning to wish that her husband wasn't quite so loud and bumptious. She had caught sight of a few astonished glances, and a few sly smiles. She wondered if she had put on too much jewellery?

She had. She 'dripped with diamonds', as June said to Susan. 'I'm only surprised she doesn't have a diamond nose-ring, as well as all the rest,' said June. 'I've a good mind to suggest it to Jo. She could pass on the idea, perhaps.'

'No, don't,' said Susan, afraid of June's unkind wit. 'She can't help having such parents. Oh, isn't her father dreadful this time?'

He really was. He had cornered Miss Parker, Jo's form mistress, and was blaring at her in his fog-horn voice.

'Well, Miss Parker – how's our Jo getting along? Naughtiest girl in the form as usual? Ah, well – they're always the most popular, aren't they? The things *I* used to do as a boy. My name's Charlie, so they called me Cheeky Charlie at school! The things I said to my teachers! Ha ha ha!'

Miss Parker made no reply. She merely looked disgusted. Jo felt frightened. She knew that face of Miss Parker's. She had a feeling that Miss Parker might say something that even Cheeky Charlie wouldn't like.

Her father went blundering on. 'Well, you haven't said a word about our Jo. She's a card, isn't she? Ha ha – I bet she calls you Nosey Parker!' And he actually gave Miss Parker a dig in the ribs!

'I have nothing to say about Jo except that she apparently takes after her father,' said Miss Parker, scarlet with annoyance. She turned away to speak to Darrell's mother, who had come to her rescue. Everyone always hoped to be rescued from Mr. Jones!

'Daddy! You shouldn't have said that,' said Jo, in great distress. 'That was *awful*. You made her angry. Please don't say things like that.'

'Well, I like *that*!' said Mr. Jones, tipping his hat back on his head and scratching the top of his forehead. 'What did I say? Oh – I was being old Cheeky Charlie again, was I? Well, you do call her Nosey Parker, don't you? My word, there's your Head. I must have a word with *her*!'

Jo tried to pull him back, and cast an agonized glance at her mother. Jo was beginning to realize that her father hadn't very good manners. Why, why, why did he shout so, why did he *always* have such a bright red shiny face, why did he poke people in the ribs and tell silly jokes? Why did he barge in on people when they were talking together, and interrupt them?

He was doing that now. Jo hadn't been able to prevent him from going right up to the little group in which the Head Mistress stood, talking to three or four parents. Her mother was blushing red. She too knew that 'Cheeky Charlie' was not at his best.

'Hallo, hallo, hallo!' said Mr. Jones, walking right into the middle of the group, and holding out a great red hand to Miss Grayling. 'You're like the Queen of England today, aren't you – holding court, with us poor parents as subjects! Ha ha ha!'

Mr. Jones was so pleased with this brilliant remark that he was quite overcome, and beamed round, expecting much approval and admiration.

He got none. Miss Grayling shook hands politely and

then dropped Mr. Jones's great paw immediately. 'How do you do?' she murmured, and turned back to the parent she was speaking to. Not one of them looked at Mr. Jones, but Cheeky Charlie had a very thick skin and didn't notice things like that.

'I hope our Jo's a credit to her school,' he began again. 'Her pa wasn't! He was a naughty boy, he was – always at the bottom of the form, wasn't he, Ma? Well, the school's looking fine, Miss Grayling!'

'Thank you,' said Miss Grayling. 'I'm afraid I must ask you to excuse me for a few minutes, whilst I finish my talk to Dr. and Mrs. Leyton.'

Mrs. Jones pulled at his arm. 'Come away, Charlie,' she begged, thinking that her husband must really have got a touch of sunstroke. He always did behave like this, of course, and shout and boast – but somehow it didn't show so much at home, among his own friends. Here it suddenly seemed very vulgar and out of place.

Mr. Jones was about to address a few hearty words to Dr. Leyton, when he caught an extraordinarily icy look in that distinguished-looking gentleman's eye. It reminded Cheeky Charlie of one of his old headmasters who had once told him exactly what he thought of him. Mr. Jones backed away, mumbling something.

Miss Grayling sighed with relief. 'I'm sorry,' she said to the other parents. 'It was an experiment, taking Jo – but I'm afraid it's not an experiment that's going to work out well. We've had other experiments before, as you know – taking girls that don't really fit in, hoping they will, later. And so far they always have done, in a marvellous way. I think Jo would too, if only she got a little backing from her parents. But her father always undoes any good we do here for Jo!'

'Let's go to another part of the grounds,' said one of the other parents in the group. 'I feel it would be safer!'

Jo was relieved to see the Head going off in another direction. Oh dear – she really would have to take her father in hand and tell him a few things. She looked rather downcast and her father squeezed her arm. 'What's up, old lady?' he said, in a kindly voice. 'Cheer up! I don't like to see my little Jo not smiling. Her old dad would do anything in the world for her!'

Jo cheered up at the love in his voice. Blow Miss Parker and Miss Grayling and everyone else! It was half-term and nobody should spoil it. She pulled at her mother's arm.

'Mother! Can I ask Deirdre, my friend, to come and be with us today? Her father's at sea and she's got no mother. So she's alone today.'

'Yes, you ask her,' said her father in his booming voice, before her mother could answer. 'We'll give her a slap-up time. I'm glad you've got a friend at last, Jo! You never seemed to have one before.'

So Deirdre was asked to join the Jones's, and was pleased to have someone to go out with, though Mr. Jones really scared her with his loud, booming voice and jovial ways.

'So you're my Jo's friend, are you?' he boomed at her. 'Well, you stick by my Jo, she's worth it, my Jo is. What's your name? Deirdre? Well, we'll send you some stunning parcels, won't we, Ma? You stick by Jo, Deirdre!'

'Yes,' stammered Deirdre, almost deafened.

'What about that money Auntie sent you the other week?' inquired Mrs. Jones, as soon as she could get a word in. 'We never heard if you got it. Have you got it safe?'

Jo hesitated. She was afraid to tell her mother that she had dropped it, and that Matron had it, and that she, Jo, hadn't dared to go and get it back. If her father knew that, he would go right up to Matron and demand the money then and there, for his precious Jo! That was simply unthinkable.

'It's quite safe,' muttered Jo, and racked her brains to think how to change the subject.

'Oh well – if you've got that money untouched, I won't give you any more at present,' said her mother. 'Twenty-five pounds is enough to keep in your drawer, or wherever you keep it. You can write if you want any more.'

Jo didn't know what to say. She had hoped her mother would give her more money – then she wouldn't need to go poking about in Matron's room for hers. Poor Jo hadn't screwed up her courage even to peep inside Matron's room yet. She had no money at all except for a few coins left from her week's pocket-money – handed out by Matron.

Half-term flashed by. The parents departed by car and train, except for Bill's father and mother, who came and went on horseback, much to Bill's delight and Clarissa's. Their half-term had been spent in riding over the cliffs, the horses enjoying the half-term as much as anyone!

'My last half-term gone,' mourned Darrell. 'Now I'm facing my very last few weeks!'

'Cheer up!' said Alicia. 'A lot can happen in a few weeks.' She was right. A lot did happen – and most of it was really very unexpected!

16 A row – and a trick

The first thing that happened was the row between June and Amanda. Most people had thought the two would blow up sooner or later, and they did!

It was over quite a simple thing. Amanda was coaching June at tennis, sending her fast serves to take – so fast and hard that June was half scared of some of them! But she slammed them back valiantly, pleased at being able to handle such terrific serves.

'June! Use your head!' shouted Amanda, stopping her serves for a minute. 'What's the good of returning these fast serves if you don't put the ball somewhere where I've got to run for it! Or even somewhere that I can't reach! All you do is to put them back right at my feet.'

'It's as much as I can do to take the serves, let alone *place* the return ball,' answered June. 'Give me a chance! Also, the court is a bit bumpy this end, and the ball doesn't bounce true. It puts me off when that happens.'

'Don't make excuses,' said Amanda.

'I'm not!' yelled June, indignantly. But Amanda was already throwing the ball high in the air for her next serve.

The ball flew like lightning over the net to June. Again it bounced on an uneven bit and swerved a little to the right. June lashed at it wildly.

It flew straight up into the air, and then swerved right over the netting round the court, landing in the middle of a watching group, who fell all over themselves trying to catch the ball, shrieking with laughter.

'If you fool about, June, we'll stop,' said Amanda, honestly thinking that June had hit the ball wildly on purpose. Something immediately went 'ping' inside June, as it always did when she lost her temper.

She didn't lose it outwardly at first. She merely collected up the balls round the court, and then sent them all flying over the surrounding netting into the watching girls, one after another.

'I'm finished,' she announced to Amanda. 'It's impossible to work with you. I shan't turn up for this sort of thing any more. It's not worth my while. So long!'

And under the admiring eyes of the watching girls, June strolled off the court, whistling softly.

Amanda called to her. 'Don't be a fool, June. Come back at once.'

June took no notice. She whistled a little more loudly, and began throwing her racket up into the air and catching it deftly as it came down. She did a few imaginary strokes with it, and then began to fool. The watching girls laughed.

Amanda strode after June. 'June! I told you to come back. If you don't, I'll see you're not chosen for even the third team.'

'Don't want to be!' said June, throwing her racket up into the air again and catching it. 'You go and find some other second-former to bawl at and chivy round. Don't waste that nice kind nature of yours, Amanda.'

And this time she really did go off, having given Amanda a look of such scorn and dislike that Amanda was shocked. The little group of spectators were scared now. They dispersed, whispering. What a bit of news to spread round the school. What a row. And wasn't June

MARVELLOUS! 'Honestly!' whispered the first and second-formers. 'Honestly she doesn't care for anyone, not even Amanda!'

Amanda told Sally, Darrell and Moira the news herself. 'June flew into a temper and the coaching is off,' she announced. 'I'm not giving up any more of my time to that ungrateful little beast. I'm sorry I gave her any now. But she would have been well worth it.'

'Oh, what a pity!' said Sally. 'We had arranged to watch June swimming tomorrow, and playing tennis the next day, to see if she could go into the second team, as you suggested. She's already good enough for the third. She could have been in all the matches!'

'Well, she can't be,' said Amanda, and then she spoke spitefully. 'She's gone off her game this week. She doesn't deserve to be in the third team either.'

Alicia spoke to June about it. 'What happened?' she said. 'Couldn't you have stuck it for a bit longer? We were going to come and watch you swimming and playing tennis this week – meaning to put you into the second teams, so that you could play in the matches.'

'I'm not going to be chivied about by anyone,' said June. 'Least of all by Amanda. Not even for the sake of shining in the second teams with the fourth and fifth-formers!'

'But, June – aren't you rather cutting off your nose to spite your face?' asked Alicia. 'Don't you *want* to play in the matches? They're important, you know. We do want to win them this year. We lost the tennis shield last year, and were only second in the swimming matches.'

June hesitated. She *did* want to play in the matches. She *would* have liked to bring honour and glory to the teams – and yes, to Malory Towers too. June was really beginning at times to see that one should play for one's side and not always for oneself.

'Well,' she said at last, 'I'll be honest with you, Alicia. Yes, I *was* looking forward to playing in the matches, and I was pretty certain I'd be chosen. But Amanda is a slave-driver and nothing else – she made me slave and she got good results – but she's so absolutely in*human*. I couldn't stick her one moment more, even if it meant giving up the matches.'

'Although you knew you might help the school to get back the tennis shield and win the swimming?' said Alicia.

There was a pause. 'I'm sorry about that,' said June, with an effort. 'I didn't think enough about that side of the question, I'm afraid. But look, Alicia – it's done now, and I'm not going back on my word. I'm fed up to the teeth with tennis and swimming. I don't want to touch a racket again this term, and if I go into the pool, I shall just fool about.'

'You'll fool about all your life, I expect,' said Alicia, getting up. 'All you think about is yourself and your own feelings. I'm sorry about it, June. You're my cousin, and I'd like to have cheered myself hoarse for once, watching you do something fine – like Darrell cheers Felicity.'

She walked off and left June feeling rather small and uncomfortable. But nothing, nothing, nothing would make June go to Amanda again. Nothing in this world. June gritted her white even teeth and swung an imaginary racket into the air and caught it. Finish! No more coaching!

Nora came running up. 'Was that Alicia? You didn't

tell her we were going to play the magnet trick on Mam'zelle Dupont today, did you?'

'Don't be an ass,' said June, scornfully. 'Do you suppose I'd split after we said we wouldn't say a word?'

'Oh. Well, you seemed to be having such a confab,' said Nora. 'I came to ask if I could have the magnet. I've been waiting ages to ask you. Was Alicia rowing you?'

'No,' said June, shortly. 'Don't be so jolly inquisitive, and mind your own business. Here's the magnet.'

Nora took it, beaming. She felt proud of being chosen by the second-formers to play the trick up in the grand sixth form. She had planned everything very carefully, with Felicity's help.

'I popped into the sixth form and took one of the exercise books off the desk,' Felicity had told Nora. 'All you've got to do is to walk into the room, apologize, and ask Mam'zelle if the book belongs to a sixth-former. You can do the trick whilst she's examining it.'

It sounded easy. Nora was thrilled when the time came that afternoon. The second-formers were free, but the upper forms were busy with work. Nora sped up to the sixth form with the book.

She heard the drone of someone reading aloud in French as she got there. She knocked at the door. Mam'zelle's voice came at once. '*Entrez*!'

Nora went in with the book. 'Excuse me, Mam'zelle,' she said, holding out the book. 'But does this belong to one of the sixth-formers?'

Mam'zelle took the book and looked at it. 'Ah – it is Mary-Lou's missing book,' she said. Behind her Nora was holding the powerful little magnet two inches away from Mam'zelle's neat little bun of hair.

Alicia's sharp eyes caught her action and she stared, hardly believing her eyes. All Mam'zelle's hair-pins at once attached themselves to the magnet. Nora withdrew it hastily, said 'Thank you, Mam'zelle' and shot out of the room before she burst into laughter. Alicia felt sure she could hear the little monkey snorting in the corridor as she fled back to the second-formers.

Mam'zelle seemed to have felt something. She usually wore more pins in her hair than Mam'zelle Rougier, and probably she had felt them all easing their way out! She put up her hand – and immediately her bun uncoiled itself and flapped down her back!

'*Tiens!*' said Mam'zelle, surprised. The girls all looked up. Alicia felt like a first-former again, longing to gulp with laughter. Mam'zelle patted her hand over her head to find her hair-pins. She could find none.

'*Que c'est drôle, ça?*' said Mam'zelle. 'How strange it is!'

She stood up and looked on the floor, wondering if, for some extraordinary reason, her pins had all fallen down there. No, they hadn't. Mam'zelle grovelled on hands and knees and looked under her desk to make certain.

The girls began to laugh. Alicia had quickly enlightened them as to what had happened. The sight of poor Mam'zelle groping about on the floor for hair-pins that were not there, her hair hanging over one shoulder, was too much even for the staid sixth-formers.

Mam'zelle stood up, looking disturbed. She continued her frenzied hunt for the missing pins. She thought possibly they might have fallen down her neck. She stood and wriggled, hoping that some would fall out. She groped round her collar, her face wearing a most bewildered expression.

She saw the girls laughing. 'You are bad wicked girls!' she said. 'Who has taken my hair-pins? They are gone. Ah, this is a strange and puzzling thing.'

'Most piggy-hoo-leeearrrr,' said Suzanne's voice.

'But nobody could have taken your pins, Mam'zelle,' said Darrell. 'Why, not one of us has come up to your desk this afternoon.'

'Ça, c'est vrai,' said Mam'zelle, and she looked alarmed. 'That is true. This is not a treek, then. My pins have vanished themselves from my hair. Girls, girls, can you see them anywhere?'

This was the signal for a frantic hunt in every ridiculous nook and cranny. Darrell was laughing helplessly, unable to keep order. For three or four minutes the sixth-formers really might have been back in the second form. Irene produced several explosions, and even the dour Amanda went off into fits of laughter.

'Girls, girls! Please!' Mam'zelle besought them. 'Miss Williams is next door. What will she think?'

Miss Williams thought quite a lot. She wondered what in the world was happening in the usually quiet sixth form. Mam'zelle got up. 'I go to make my bun again,' she said, and disappeared in a dignified but very hurried manner.

17 Jo and Deirdre

The girls laughed and laughed. 'It was that little monkey of a Nora,' said Alicia, again. 'I saw the magnet in her hand. The cheek of it – a second-former coming right up into our room.'

'Terribly funny though,' said Clarissa, wiping her tears away. 'I haven't laughed so much for terms. I wish Nora would do it again, with me *looking*!'

'Poor Mam'zelle – she was absolutely bewildered,' said Mary-Lou.

'*Ah ça – c'est très très* piggy-hoo-leeeearr,' said Suzanne, enjoying the joke thoroughly. 'Vairy, vairy, piggy-hoo-leeearrrrr. Most scrumpleeeeecious!'

Mam'zelle had shot into the little workroom she shared with Miss Potts, the first-form mistress. Miss Potts was mildly surprised to see Mam'zelle appear so suddenly with her hair down her back – not more than mildly though, because in her years with Mam'zelle Miss Potts had become used to various 'piggy-hoo-leeeearrr' behaviour at times from Mam'zelle.

'Miss Potts! All my pins have went!' said Mam'zelle, her grammar going too.

'Pins? What pins?' said Miss Potts. 'You don't mean your hair-pins, do you? How could they go?'

'That I do not know,' said Mam'zelle, staring at Miss Potts with such tragic eyes that Miss Potts wanted to laugh. 'One moment my bun, he is there on top – the next he is all undone. And when I look for his pins, they are gone.'

This sounded like a trick to Miss Potts, and she said so.

'No, no, Miss Potts,' asserted Mam'zelle. 'Not one girl left her place to come to me this afternoon, not one.'

'Oh well,' said Miss Potts, dismissing the matter as one of the many unaccountable things that so often seemed to happen to Mam'zelle, 'I expect you didn't put enough pins in, so your bun just came down.'

Mam'zelle found some pins and pinned her bun up so firmly that it really looked very peculiar. But she wasn't taking any risks this time! She went back to the class-room, with her dignity restored.

Nora recounted what she had done, when she got back to the second-formers. They laughed. 'I bet the sixth got a laugh when Mam'zelle's bun descended!' said June. 'It's a pity you couldn't stay and see.'

The first sixth-former they saw was the French girl, Suzanne. She came hurrying up to them, smiling.

'Ah, you bad Nora!' she cried, and went off into a stream of excited French. Susan, who was good at French, translated swiftly, and the second-formers laughed in delight at the vivid description of Mam'zelle's astonishment and dismay.

'Clarissa said she wished you would do it again, when she was looking,' said Suzanne, in French. 'We would like to see it done. Me also, I would like it very much. *We* are too big and old and prudent to do tricks – but we do not mind watching *you*!'

This was very naughty of Suzanne. No sixth-former would be silly enough to encourage the younger ones to come and play tricks in their room as much as they liked – which was what Suzanne was telling them to do! But

Suzanne was French. She hadn't quite the same ideas of responsibility that the British girls had.

She was often bored with lessons, and longed for 'peefle' of some kind. If the second-formers would provide some, that would be '*Magnifique*! *Superbe*!'

'Right,' said June at once. 'If that's what you want, it shall be done. I'll think up a little something for the entertainment of the sixth.'

June was bored now that she had practically given up playing games or swimming properly. She was in the mood for wickedness and mischief of some kind – and what better than this? She set her sharp brains to work at once.

Jo was aggrieved at not having been told that the hair-pin trick was to be played by Nora in the sixth form. 'You *might* have told me,' she said. 'You always leave me out.'

'You tell everything to that first-form baby – what's her name – Deirdre,' said June. 'That's why we don't let you into our secrets.'

'I've a good mind to share my parcel that came today with the first form, instead of with *you*,' said Jo.

'Do,' said June. 'Probably you can buy their liking and their friendship with food. Unfortunately you can't buy ours. A pity – but there it is!'

Jo was miserable. She *was* beginning to understand that heaps of money and sweets and food didn't in the least impress the girls. But perhaps if she gave a most wonderful midnight feast on her birthday, and asked them all to it and was very modest and friendly herself, they might think she was not too bad after all?

But how could she buy a grand feast without money?

She brooded over the money that Matron had of hers. She still hadn't claimed it.

'And if I do, she won't give it to me,' Jo wailed to Deirdre for the twentieth time. 'I *must* screw up my courage, snoop into her room, and see if I can spot where she's put my money.'

A most unexpected opportunity suddenly came. Matron sent a message by Susan to say she wanted Jo.

Jo went pale. 'What for?' she asked.

'Don't know,' said Susan. 'Probably you've mended your red gloves with blue wool again. You must think Matron's colour blind when you keep doing things like that!'

Jo went off dolefully. She felt absolutely certain that Matron was going to ask her if the twenty-five pounds was hers. She felt it in her bones!

She found the door of Matron's room open, and went in. There was nobody there. From far down the corridor she could hear yells. Somebody must have fallen down and hurt themselves and Matron had rushed off to give first aid. Jo took a quick look round the familiar room. Ugh, the bottles of medicine!

There was no money to be seen anywhere – but suddenly Jo saw something that made her stand stock-still.

Matron had a small, heavy safe in the corner of the room, into which she locked what money she had – the girls' pocket-money, the doctor's fees, and so on. To Jo's enormous surprise, the safe door was a little open, the keys hanging from the keyhole! Obviously Matron had just been about to open or shut the safe when she had heard the agonized yells. She had rushed out, forgetting the keys left in the safe door.

Jo ran to the door and peered out. Not a soul was there. She ran back to the safe and opened the door. There was a pile of notes on one shelf, and a pile of silver on the next. Jo grabbed some notes, stuffed them into her pocket and fled!

No one saw her go. Not a soul did she meet as she raced back. She went to find Deirdre and they shut themselves into one of the bathrooms and locked the door.

'Look,' said Jo, pulling the money out of the pocket. 'Nobody was in Matron's office. I've got my money back.'

'But Jo – there's more than twenty-five pounds there!' said Deirdre.

So there was. There were nine five-pound notes, all new and clean.

'Gosh – I didn't think there were so many,' said Jo. 'Never mind. I'll borrow the extra four! I can easily get Daddy to send me four fivers when I next write to him, and then I'll put them back.'

'Wouldn't it – wouldn't it be called stealing if we don't put them back at once?' asked Deirdre, scared.

Jo was so frightened that Deirdre might ask her to return them to Matron's room, that she pooh-poohed this suggestion at once. She felt sure she would be caught if she went to put them back!

'No, of course not,' she said. 'Don't be silly. I've always plenty of money. I don't need to *steal*, do I? I tell you, twenty-five pounds of this is my own money and four fivers I've just borrowed – and I'll pay them back next week.'

Deirdre cheered up. 'Shall we go and buy things for the feast now?' she asked. 'Gosh, what a lot we can get! We'll go over to the town, shall we, next time we're allowed out, and buy stacks of things!'

Jo was very cock-a-hoop now. She felt she had done a very fine and daring thing. She got two safety-pins and pinned the notes safely in the pocket of her blouse, afraid that she might lose them again.

The two of them set out the next day to go shopping. 'Where shall we hide the stuff?' said Jo. 'I daren't put it anywhere in the dormy, and the common-room's not safe.'

'Well, it's very fine weather. We could really hide it under a hedge somewhere,' said Deirdre.

They bought a great many things. Packets of biscuits, tins of Nestlé's milk, tins of sardines, chocolate bars by the dozen, bags of sweets, tins of peaches and pears! They staggered out with half the things, promising to go back for the others. They had kit bags with them, but these didn't hold half the goods.

They found a good place in a field to hide the food. An old tree stump had fallen down, covering a hollow beneath it. The girls stuffed everything into the little hollow, which was perfectly dry. They went back for the rest of the things.

They paid the bill – twenty-five pounds! Deirdre could hardly believe her ears. It was more money than she had had to spend in five years!

'We've got good value for the money though,' said Jo, as they staggered off again, laden with tins and packages. 'There's enough and more for every one of the twenty-three girls in the form!'

They hid the second lot of food, strewed ivy strands over the opening to the hollow, and went back to school, well pleased with themselves. They had decided to ask a dozen or so of the second-formers to go with them to retrieve the food later on. They were sure they could never manage to take it all the way to school without falling by the wayside!

But, before anyone could be told about the exciting array of goods, Jo got into trouble. She was supposed to go out for walks only with another second-former or with someone of a higher form. The first-formers only went for walks accompanied by a sixth-former or by a mistress, though the rule was sometimes disregarded. Jo had broken it by taking a first-former out – and she had also brought Deirdre back an hour too late for her prep.

So that evening Miss Parker, the second-form mistress, gave Jo a shock. She rapped on her desk, after a note had been brought in to her, and everyone looked up from their prep.

'I have here a note,' said Miss Parker. 'It informs me that Deirdre Barker, of the first form, was taken out this afternoon by a second-former – which is against the rules – and did not return until an hour after prep was started in the first form. Deirdre has not given the name of the second-former. I must therefore ask her to stand up so that I may see who it is.'

Everyone knew it was Jo, of course. They had seen her go off with Deirdre, and even if they hadn't they would have guessed it was Jo, Deirdre's friend. One or two looked at Jo expectantly.

And Jo was afraid of owning up! She was afraid of having to say where they had been, and what they had bought, and where the money had come from. She trembled in her seat, and kept her eyes down. Her cheeks grew crimson. Miss Parker waited for two minutes in silence.

'Very well,' she said. 'If the culprit will not own up, I must punish the whole class. The second form will not go swimming for three days.'

18 Running away

Still Jo did not stand up. She couldn't. Oh, the girls didn't understand! It wasn't just owning up to taking Deirdre out without permission, it was all the other things that might be found out – that forty-five pounds for instance!

Forty-five pounds. FORTY-FIVE POUNDS. It suddenly began to loom bigger and bigger and bigger. Why had she taken it? Just to get her own money back, and out of bravado too – to impress Deirdre. Jo kept her head down for the rest of prep, but she was quite unable to do any work at all.

The storm broke in the dormy that night.

'Jo! What do you mean by not owning up?' demanded June. 'You go down and own up immediately. Go on!'

'It wasn't me with Deirdre,' said Jo, feebly.

'Oh, JO! You're worse than ever. How can you tell lies like that?' cried Felicity. 'Go down and own up. You don't really mean to say you're going to have the whole form docked of its swimming for three days? You must be mad!'

'All right, I'm mad then,' said Jo, feeling like a hunted animal when she saw all the angry, accusing faces turned towards her.

'You're not fit to be at Malory Towers,' said Susan, in a cutting voice. 'I can't think why you ever came. You're getting worse instead of better.'

'Don't,' said Jo, her eyes filling with tears.

'That's right – cry!' said Katherine. 'You deserve to. Now, for the last time, are you going to own up or not?'

'I wasn't with Deirdre,' repeated Jo, obstinately.

'We shall send you to Coventry,' said June. 'We shall not speak to you, any of us, or have anything to do with you for three whole weeks. See? That's the kind of punishment that is kept specially for people who behave like you, Josephine Jones – people who let others be punished for what they have done themselves, and then are too cowardly to stop it. We shan't speak to you for three weeks!'

'But – it's my birthday soon – and I've got a feast for everyone!' cried Jo, wildly.

'You'll be the only one at your feast,' said June, grimly. 'Unless you like to ask that drip of a Deirdre. Now it's understood, isn't it, everyone? From this moment Jo is in Coventry!'

Jo hadn't heard of being sent to Coventry before. It was new to her. It meant that not a single person spoke to her, answered her, or even looked at her. She might not have been there for all the notice they took of her that night. Jo cried in bed. *Why* hadn't she given up that money to Matron as soon as she had had it from her aunt? That was when all the trouble had begun.

She waited till the others were asleep and then went to find Deirdre. The two crept together into the corridor to whisper. 'Deirdre – I can't stand it,' wept Jo. 'I shall run away. I want to go home. Everyone's so unkind to me here. Except you.'

'I shouldn't have come shopping with you,' whispered Deirdre. 'I'm the cause of all the trouble.'

'Oh, Deirdre – will you come with me if I run away?' asked Jo, sniffing. 'I'd be afraid to go alone. Please, please say you'll come with me.'

Deirdre hesitated. The idea of running away scared her – but she was very weak and easily led. Jo was much the stronger of the two and Jo had been very generous to her.

'All right. I'll come too,' she said, and immediately Jo cheered up. They began to plan.

'I tell you what we'll do,' said Jo. 'We'll take all that food of ours to that shack we passed on a long country walk we went on last term – do you remember? The first and second-formers went together and we all played in the shack. It was in a very lonely place. We'll take the food there, and we can stay there a day or two before trying to find the way home.'

This seemed rather a delightful adventure to Deirdre. She agreed at once. 'We'd better get up early tomorrow,' she said, 'and go and take the stuff to and fro. It will take us two journeys at least, and it's quite a long way to that shack.'

Jo felt quite cheerful now. What would the second-formers feel like when they knew that sending her to

Coventry had made her run away? Jo didn't think of the worry she would cause the school and her parents by disappearing suddenly. She was completely selfish, and soon began to view the whole thing in the guise of a wonderful escapade.

Somehow or other she managed to wake the next morning very early. She dressed and woke Deirdre, whose bed was fortunately beside the door in her dormy. The two set off quietly. They came at last to the hollow where they had hidden their goods, and then began the long trek to and fro to the shack. It took them longer than they imagined. The shack was a good place to hide in. It was a long long way from any road, and only a bridle path led anywhere near it. No one, except for a few hikers, usually came near it.

'There,' said Jo, pleased, putting down the last tin of peaches. 'We must remember to bring a tin-opener. We've really got enough food to last for weeks, Deirdre.'

'We ought to get back quickly,' said Deirdre, looking at her watch. 'We'll be awfully late for breakfast – and whatever we do we mustn't be seen coming in together again.'

'Nobody's spotted us at all so far,' said Jo. 'We're lucky.'

It was true that nobody had recognized them. But somebody had seen them, far away in the distance! Bill, on her horse Thunder, and Clarissa, on Merrylegs, were out for one of their early morning rides, and had followed a bridle path not far distant from the shack. Bill's sharp eyes caught sight of two figures going into the shack.

'Funny!' she said. 'That looks like two Malory Towers

123

girls – same uniform. Perhaps it's two out for an early morning walk.'

'Probably,' said Clarissa, and thought no more about it. They galloped on, and had a wonderful ride, getting back just before Jo and Deirdre – who were careful to slip in at different gates.

They had planned to run away that night, when all the others were asleep in bed. The second-formers were surprised at Jo's behaviour that day. They had expected her to be miserable and subdued, because being ignored completely was a very hard punishment – but instead Jo was bright-eyed and cheerful, seeming not to care in the least about being sent to Coventry.

'She's a thick-skinned little beast,' said June to Felicity. June was doing a double dose of ignoring. She was not only ignoring Jo, she was ignoring Amanda! It so happened that they met quite a number of times during those few days and June took great delight in turning her back on Amanda in a very marked manner.

That night, when the girls in the second-form dormy were fast asleep, Jo got up and dressed very quietly. She took the rug off her bed, and then stole into Deirdre's dormy. Deirdre was awake, half afraid now that the time had come. For two pins she would have given up the idea entirely!

But Jo had no idea of giving it up or of allowing Deirdre to either! It wasn't long before both of them were stealing down the moonlit corridor, each with their rug over their arm. It was easy to open the garden door and go out into the grounds.

'I'm glad it's moonlight,' said Deirdre, with a half-scared laugh. 'I wouldn't like to go on a dark night. Oh,

Jo – you're sure it's all right? You're sure your people won't mind my turning up with you?'

'Oh no. They'll welcome you as my friend,' said Jo. 'And they'll laugh at our adventure, I know they will. They'll think it's wonderful!'

They got to the shack at last. All their food was still there. They spread the rugs on the floor and lay down to sleep. It was quite warm, but for some time neither of them could sleep. In the end Jo broke open a packet of biscuits and they munched steadily. Deirdre fell asleep first, and then Jo found her eyes closing.

What would the girls think tomorrow? They'd be sorry they'd driven her away! thought Jo. Miss Parker would be sorry for the nasty things she had said. So would Mam'zelle. So would . . . But Jo was now fast asleep, and never even heard a little hedgehog scuttling across the floor of the shack.

Nobody took any notice of the girls' empty beds in the morning. It was quite usual for someone to get up early for a walk or a swim. The first and second-formers clattered down to breakfast, chattering as usual.

But before long, the news went round the school. 'Jo's gone! Deirdre's gone! Nobody knows where they are. They've hunted everywhere for them!'

The second-formers couldn't help feeling rather guilty. Had their punishment sent Jo off? No – she had so very very often said she would run away! All the same – perhaps she had run away because she couldn't stand being sent to Coventry – and taken weak little Deirdre with her. What would happen? Where on earth had they gone to?

The police were told. Miss Grayling rang up Mr.

Jones and informed him that his daughter was missing, but they hoped to find her, and also a girl she had taken with her, at any moment. They couldn't have gone far.

Miss Grayling was amazed at Mr. Jones's reception of her news. She had expected him to be upset and worried, perhaps to reproach the school for not taking more care of Jo. But down the telephone came a bellow of laughter.

'Ha, ha, ha! If that isn't exactly like our Jo! She's just like me, you know. The times I played truant from school! Don't you worry about our Jo, Miss Grayling. She knows how to look after herself all right. Maybe she's on her way home. I'll telephone you if she arrives.'

'Mr. Jones – the police have been informed,' said Miss Grayling, disgusted at the way Jo's father had taken her news. 'I will try to keep it out of the papers as long as I can, of course.'

'Oh, don't you bother about *that*,' said the surprising Mr. Jones. 'I'd like to see our Jo hitting the headlines in a spot of adventure. Great girl, isn't she?'

He was surprised to hear the click of the receiver being put down firmly at Miss Grayling's end. 'What's the matter with *her*?' he wondered. 'Cutting me off like that. Hey, Ma – where are you? What do you think our Jo's done?'

A very disturbing piece of news came to Miss Grayling that morning. It came from the police sergeant who had been told of the missing girls. After Miss Grayling had spoken about them and given their descriptions, the sergeant cleared his throat and spoke rather awkwardly.

'Er – about that other matter you reported a short while ago, Miss Grayling,' he said. 'The notes that were stolen from your Matron's safe. You remember Matron knew the numbers printed on the notes – they were in a sequence. Well, we've traced them.'

'Oh,' said Miss Grayling. 'Do you know who the thief is, then?'

'Well, Mam, yes, in a way we do,' said the sergeant. 'Those notes were given in at two shops in the town, by a Malory Towers girl. She came in with another girl and bought a whole lot of food – tins and tins of it.'

Miss Grayling's heart sank. She covered her eyes. Not a *Malory Towers* girl! Could there possibly be a thief like that among the girls?

'Thank you, sergeant,' she said at last. 'I will make enquiries as to which girls they were. Good morning.'

19 A dreadful morning for Jo

It was soon quite clear that it was Jo and Deirdre who had done the shopping. Everything came out bit by bit. Matron told how she found the five-pound notes and knew that they belonged to Jo. Jo had never claimed them.

The second-formers related that Jo meant to buy food for a birthday feast. Miss Parker added the bit about Deirdre going out with a second-former, and how she had not been able to make that second-former own up.

'But,' she said, 'there is no doubt at all but that it was Jo.'

'Yes,' said Miss Grayling, seeing the whole miserable story now. Jo had gone to Matron's room to get back her own money and had taken more than she meant to – and then had been too afraid to put it back. Then trouble had come, and fear and misery had caused Jo to run away. Silly, ill-brought-up, spoiled little Jo!

'Mostly her parents' fault, of course,' said Miss Grayling to Matron. 'Nothing to be done there, I'm afraid. They're no help to her.'

There was a knock at the door. Bill and Clarissa were outside.

They had remembered the two figures they had seen near the old shack the morning before. Could they have been Jo and Deirdre?

'Quite likely,' said Miss Grayling. 'They may have hidden their food there, and be camping out. Do you know the way?'

'Oh *yes*,' said Bill. 'We often ride out there. We thought it would really be quickest for us to ride out on Thunder and Merrylegs, Miss Grayling, and see if the two girls *are* there.'

'Miss Peters can go too, on her horse,' said Miss Grayling. 'If the girls are there, she can bring them back.'

So the three riders set off, and rode over the fields and hills till they came to the bridle path that led near the shack. Jo and Deirdre, sitting inside the shack, having their fourth 'snack' that morning, heard the hooves. Deirdre peeped out.

'It's Bill and Clarissa,' she said, darting back, looking scared. 'And Miss Peters.'

'They can't guess we're here,' said Jo, in a panic.

But they *had* guessed, of course, and very soon the three of them dismounted, and Miss Peters walked to the shack. She looked inside. She saw Jo and Deirdre, looking very dirty and untidy and frightened, crouching in a corner.

'So there you are,' she said. 'What a pair of idiots. Come out, at once, please. We've had enough of this nonsense.'

Like two frightened puppies, Jo and Deirdre crept out of the shed. Bill and Clarissa looked at them.

'So it *was* you we saw yesterday,' said Bill. 'What are you playing at? Red Indians or something?'

'Bill! Shall we get into awful trouble?' asked Deirdre, looking rather white. She had not enjoyed the night in the shack. A wind had blown in, and she had felt cold in the early morning. She had awakened and had not been able to sleep again. Also there seemed to be rather a nasty smell of some sort in the shack – perhaps it was mice, thought Deirdre, who was terrified of them.

Bill looked at the pale Deirdre and felt sorry for her. She was only a first-former, just thirteen years old, and a timid, weak little thing – just the type that Jo *would* pick on to boast to, and persuade to do wrong.

'Look, Deirdre – you've been an idiot, and you might have caused a lot of worry and trouble, if it hadn't happened that Clarissa and I spotted you the other day, when you were here,' said Bill. 'It's a mercy it hasn't got into the papers yet. The best thing you can do is to be absolutely straight and honest about it, and to be really sorry, and promise to turn over a new leaf. Then I dare say you'll get another chance.'

'Shall I be expelled?' asked Deirdre, panic-stricken at the thought. 'My father would be awfully upset. I haven't got a mother.'

'I shouldn't think you'd be sent away,' said Bill, kindly. 'You've not got a bad name, so far as I know. Come on now. You can get up on Thunder, behind me.'

Deirdre was frightened of horses, but she was even more frightened of disobeying Bill, and getting into further trouble. She climbed up on Thunder, and Jo was taken on Miss Peters' horse. Miss Peters said only a few words to the dirty, bedraggled Jo.

'Running away from things is never any good,' she said. 'You can't run away from difficulties. You only take them with you. Remember that, Jo. Now hang on to me and we'll go.'

They got back just about break-time. The sound of hooves was heard as they came up the drive, and the girls ran to see if Jo and Deirdre were being brought back. They looked in silence at the dirty, bedraggled, sorry-looking pair!

The two were taken straight to Miss Grayling. Deirdre was now in a state of utter panic. However *could* she have gone with Jo! What would her father say? She was all he had got, and now he would be ashamed and sorry because she had brought disgrace on the fine school he had sent her to.

Tears streamed down her cheeks, and before Miss Grayling could say a word, Deirdre poured out all she was feeling.

'Miss Grayling, I'm sorry. Don't tell my father, please, please, don't. He trusts me, and I'm all he's got. Miss Grayling, don't send me away. I'll never, never do such a thing again, I promise you. I can't think why I did it. If only you'll give me another chance, I'll do my best. Miss Grayling, please believe me!'

Miss Grayling knew real repentance when she saw it. This was not someone trying to get out of trouble, it was someone shocked by what she had done, someone thinking now of the effect it might have on somebody she loved – someone with an earnest desire to turn over a new leaf!

'I'll show you that I mean what I say,' went on Deirdre, beseechingly, rubbing away her tears with a very grubby hand, and streaking her face with dirt. 'Give me all the hard punishments you like, I'll do them. But please don't tell my father. He's a sailor, and he would *never* run away. He'd be so ashamed of me.'

'Running away never gets us anywhere,' said Miss Grayling, gravely. 'It is the coward's way. Facing up to things is the hero's way. I shall think what I am to do with you, and tell you later on in the morning. I am sure that whatever I decide you will accept, and face bravely.'

She turned and glanced at Matron, who was sitting quietly knitting in a corner of the big room.

'Will you take Deirdre now?' she said. 'She wants a bath, to begin with, and clean clothes. Don't let her go into class this morning. Give her some job to do with you, will you? When she's in a calmer state of mind I'll talk to her again.'

Matron, calm, kindly and efficient, put her knitting into her bag. 'Come along, my girl,' she said to Deirdre. 'I'll soon deal with you. I never did see such a grubby first-former in my life. A hot bath and clean clothes will make you feel a lot better. And after that you can help me to tidy out my linen cupboard. That'll keep you busy! Keep you out of mischief too!'

She took the girl's arm in a kindly way, and Deirdre heaved a sigh of relief. She was always scared of Matron, but suddenly she seemed a real rock, someone to lean on – almost like a mother, thought Deirdre, who had missed a mother very much indeed. She kept close to Matron as she hurried her away. She longed to ask her if she thought the Head would expel her, but she was afraid of the answer. Poor Deirdre. She was not meant for escapades of any sort.

Jo had been standing silent all this time, fearful of saying a word. Miss Grayling looked at her. 'I am expecting your father in ten minutes' time,' she said, 'or I would send you to have a bath too. But it would be better to wait now, till he comes.'

Jo's heart lifted. So her father would soon be here. *He* wouldn't be cross about this. It would tickle him. He would laugh and joke about it, and tell all his friends about the latest thing his Jo had done. He would put things right!

Jo heaved a sigh of relief. 'Sit down,' said Miss Grayling. 'We will discuss this miserable affair with your father when he arrives. I sent for him as soon as I heard from Bill and Clarissa that they knew where you were hiding.'

Miss Grayling began writing a letter. Jo sat still. She wished she didn't look so dirty. She had a great hole in her tunic, and her bare knees were filthy.

In ten minutes' time an enormous car roared up the drive. Daddy! thought Jo. He hasn't been long! The car came to a stop with a screeching of brakes. Someone got out and the car door was slammed loudly.

Soon Mr. Jones appeared at the sitting-room door. He came in, beaming. 'So you found that rascal, did you?' he said. 'Why, here she is! Just like you, Jo, to go off like that. She's a scamp, isn't she, Miss Grayling?'

'Won't you sit down?' said Miss Grayling, in a remarkably cool voice. 'I want to discuss this matter with you, Mr. Jones. We take a serious view of it, I am afraid. It is fortunate that it did not get into the papers.'

'Yes, but look here – what's so serious about it?' exploded Mr. Jones. 'It was just a bit of fun – Jo's a high-spirited girl – nothing wrong about her at all!'

'There is a lot wrong,' said Miss Grayling. 'So much so, Mr. Jones, that I want you to take Jo away with you today – and I regret to say that we cannot have her back. She is not a good influence in the school.'

Mr. Jones had never in his life had such a sudden and unpleasant surprise. He sat with his mouth falling open, hardly able to believe his ears. Jo – Jo expelled! They wanted him to take her away and not bring her back? Why? WHY?

Jo was shocked and horrified. She gave a gulp and stared at her father. He found his voice at last.

He began to bluster. 'Yes, but look here, you can't do that – you know it was only a bit of fun. I grant you Jo shouldn't have done it – caused a lot of trouble and all that – and she shouldn't have taken the other kid with her either. But – but you can't *expel* her for that, surely!'

'We could, Mr. Jones, if we thought she was an undesirable influence,' said Miss Grayling. 'It doesn't often happen, of course – in fact, very, very rarely. But in this case it *is* going to happen. You see – it isn't only the running away – it's a little matter of the taking of some money.'

Jo covered her face. She could have dropped through the floor. So Miss Grayling knew all about that too! Her father looked dumbfounded. He stood up and looked down at Miss Grayling, and his voice shook.

'What do you mean? You can't say my Jo is a thief! You can't! I don't believe it. She's always had *heaps* of money.'

Miss Grayling said nothing. She merely indicated Jo, who still sat with her face covered, bending forward with tears soaking between her fingers. Her father stared at her, aghast.

'Jo,' he said, in a voice that had suddenly gone hoarse. 'Jo – you didn't, oh you didn't! I can't believe it!'

Jo could only nod her head. That awful, awful money! There was still the rest of it pinned in her blouse. She could feel it rustling when she moved. She suddenly pulled it out. She put it in front of Miss Grayling. 'That's all that's left,' she said. 'But I'll pay the rest back.'

'Let me pay everything, everything – I'll double it!' said Mr. Jones, in the same hoarse voice. 'To think of Jo – my Jo – taking money!'

Both the bold brazen Jo and the once blustering bumptious man looked at Miss Grayling miserably and humbly. She was sorry for them both.

'I think there is no need to say any more,' she said, quietly. 'I don't want any explanations from Jo. You can get those from her, if you wish. But you will see, Mr. Jones, that I cannot keep Jo here any longer. She had a fine chance at Malory Towers, and she didn't take it. And I think I should say this to you – her parents are partly to

135

blame. You didn't give Jo the backing up and the help that she needed.'

'No, you didn't, Dad!' cried Jo, sobbing. 'You said it didn't matter if I was bottom of the form – YOU always were! You said I needn't bother about rules, I could break them all if I liked. You said so long as I had a good time, that was the only thing that mattered. And it wasn't, it wasn't.'

Mr. Jones stood still and silent. He turned suddenly to Miss Grayling. 'I reckon Jo's right,' he said, in a voice that sounded astonished. 'And I reckon, Miss Grayling, that you might have given Jo another chance if you'd thought *I'd* see things the right way – and I didn't. Come on, Jo – we've got to get things straight between us – come on home, now.'

He held out his hand, and Jo took it, gulping. Mr. Jones held out his hand to Miss Grayling and spoke with unexpected dignity.

'Good-bye, Miss Grayling. I reckon I'm the one that's really at fault, not Jo. You won't spread this matter about, will you – for Jo's sake? About the money, I mean.'

'Of course not,' said Miss Grayling, shaking hands. 'And Mr. Jones – however much you make a joke of the escapade to your friends, and gloss over the fact that Jo has been expelled – I do beg of you not to make a joke of it with Jo. This is a serious thing. It may be the turning-point in her life, for good or for bad – and she has a right to expect that her parents will show her the right road.'

In a few minutes' time the big car roared off down the road. Jo was gone – gone for ever from Malory Towers. One of the failures, who perhaps in the future *might* be a success, if only her parents backed her up.

How important parents are! thought Miss Grayling. Really, I think somebody should start a School for Parents too!

20 Amanda goes swimming

Deirdre was not expelled. Her real fault had been weakness, and that could be dealt with. When she heard that she was to stay on, she could have sung for joy. She was shocked about Jo, but secretly relieved to be free of her strong, dominating influence.

The whole school was shocked too. It was so very rare for any girl to be expelled – but everyone agreed that Jo was impossible.

'Poor kid,' said Mary-Lou. 'Who could be decent with idiotic parents like that – throwing money about all over the place, boasting, thick-skinned, trying to make Jo as bad as themselves. Well – it was one of Malory Towers' experiments that went wrong.'

'I must say I'd rather have a generous parent like Jo's than a mean one like mine, though,' put in Gwen. 'Jo's father would never have grudged her an extra year at a finishing school.'

'You've got a bee in your bonnet about that,' said Alicia. 'And let me tell you, it buzzes too loudly and too often. Your father's worth ten of Jo's – oh, not in money, but in the things that matter!'

'That was a very nasty business about Jo,' said Darrell. 'I'm glad it's over. Now perhaps we'll have a bit of peace without any more alarms and excursions!'

This was, of course, a foolish thing to say. Things began to happen almost immediately!

Amanda had decided that the tide would be right for her swim out to sea the next morning. She was looking forward to it eagerly. A good long swim at last!

She was in a small, sixth-form dormy, with only three others. All the others were very sound sleepers – Moira, Sally and Bill. She could easily creep out without waking them. She didn't mean to tell any of them what she was going to do, or what she had done, when she had had her long swim! They were so keen on rules being kept – but such rules, thought Amanda, really didn't apply to a future Olympic swimmer!

She got up at half-past four in the morning. It was dawn, and the sky was full of silvery light. Soon it would change to gold and pink as the sun came up. It would be a heavenly day!

She went quietly out. There wasn't a sound to be heard in the whole of the school. Amanda was soon standing by the pool, stripping off her clothes. She had on her swimming-costume underneath. She had a dip in the pool first – lovely! Her strong arms thrashed through the water, and her strong body revelled in it. She turned on her back for a few minutes and dreamed of the next year, when she would win the swimming at the Olympic Games. She pictured the crowds, she heard the roar of cheering and the sound of hundreds of people clapping.

It was a very pleasant picture. Amanda enjoyed it. Then she climbed out of the pool and made her way down to the edge of the rocks. The waves came pounding in there, although further out it was very calm. Amanda looked out to the brilliant blue sea and sky. She dived cleanly into a deep pool and swam through a channel there, and was suddenly out in the open sea.

At last! she thought, as her arms cleaved the water and her legs shot her steadily forward. At last I am really *swimming* again!

She went in the direction she had planned. The sun rose a little higher in the sky and shone down. It was going to be a hot day. Little sparkles came on the water, and Amanda laughed for joy. Splash, splash, splash – she swam on and on, part of the sea itself.

Nobody had seen her go. She planned to be back before anyone came down for an early morning swim. At the earliest that would be seven o'clock. She had plenty of time.

But someone came down *before* seven o'clock that morning. June woke up early and could not get off to sleep again. The sun shone right on her face. She glanced at her clock. Six o'clock. Gosh – ages before the dressing-bell went. She sat up and pulled her dressing-gown towards her.

I'll go down and have a swim, she thought. A real swim in the pool, not just fooling about, like I've been doing since I had that row with Amanda. I'll see if I've remembered all her rules.

She went softly down the stairs and out into the sun-drenched grounds. She was soon down by the pool, and went to find her swimming-costume, which she had left there to dry. She pulled it on. Then into the pool she went with a neat dive.

It was glorious there – and lovely to have it all to herself. Usually it was so crowded. June floated lazily. Then she began to swim. Yes – she had remembered everything that Amanda had taught her. She shot through the water at top speed, her lithe body as supple as a fish. Up and down she went, up and down, till she was tired out.

She climbed out to have a rest and sit in the sun. She decided to go down to the edge of the sea, and let the waves splash her as she sat on the rocks. So down she went, and found a high shelf of rock to sit on, where waves could just splash over her legs.

She gazed idly out to sea. What a marvellous blue – a kind of delphinium blue, June decided. And then her eyes suddenly fastened on a little black bob, some way out to sea. Could it be a buoy, fastened there to show a hidden rock? June had never noticed it before.

Then she saw what looked like a white arm raised. She leaped to her feet. Goodness gracious – it was a swimmer! Out there, caught by the current, someone was swimming desperately to prevent themselves being forced on to the rocks some way along.

June stood still, her heart suddenly beating fast. She watched intently. It *was* a swimmer, though she couldn't make out whether it was a man or a woman. Did he or she *know* the current had caught him, and was dragging him to the rocks, where waves were pounding high?

Yes. Amanda knew. Amanda felt the strong, swift current beneath her. How could she ever have laughed at it? It was stronger than ten swimmers, than twenty

140

swimmers! It pulled at her relentlessly, and no matter how she swam against it, it swept her in the opposite direction.

Amanda was very tired. Her great strength had been used for a long time now against the treacherous current of water. She saw with panic that she was being taken nearer and nearer to the rocks she had been warned against. She would have no chance if one of those great waves took her and flung her on them – she would be shattered at once!

June saw that the swimmer was trying to swim against the current. She knew it was hopeless. What could she do? Had she time to run back to school, warn someone and get them to telephone for help? No, she hadn't.

There's only one thing to do, thought June. Just one chance! The boat! If I can get to the boat-house in time, drag out the boat, and cut the swimmer off before he gets on the rocks, I might save him. Just a chance!

She tore off to the little boat-house in her swimming-costume. It was some way along the shore, in a place free of rocks and pounding waves. June found the key, unlocked the door and tried to drag out one of the little boats the girls sometimes used, when old Tom the boatman could be persuaded to take them for a row.

Even this little boat was heavy. June tugged at it and pushed – and at last it reached the water, and took off on a wave. June sprang in and caught up the oars. She began to row at top speed, but soon had to slacken, because she was so out of breath. She glanced round to spot the swimmer.

There he was – no, it must be a she, because it had longish hair, wet and draggled. What an idiot! June pulled strongly at the oars, horrified to see that the swimmer was being swept very near the rocks now.

The sea was calm, fortunately, so the waves that pounded the rocks were not so tremendous as usual. June yelled to the swimmer.

'AHOY THERE! AHOY!'

The swimmer didn't hear. Amanda was almost spent. Her arms were now hardly moving. She could fight against the current no longer.

'AHOY!' yelled June again. This time Amanda heard. She turned her head. A boat! Oh, what a blessed, beautiful sight! But could she possibly get to it, or it to her, in time?

The boat came on. A wave suddenly took Amanda strongly in its grasp, swelled up and flung her forward. A hidden rock struck her leg, and she cried out in agony.

Gosh – she's almost on the rocks, thought June, in a panic. She rowed wildly, and at last reached the swimmer, who was now allowing herself to float, unable to swim a stroke.

June reached out to her over the side of the boat. It's Amanda! she realized, with a shock of amazement. Well, who would have thought she'd be such an idiot?

Miraculously the swell subsided for a minute or two, and June pulled at Amanda. 'Come on – help yourself up!' she shouted. 'Buck up!'

How Amanda ever got into the boat she didn't know. Neither did June. It seemed impossible, for Amanda had a badly hurt leg and arm. But somehow it was done, and at last she lay in the bottom of the boat, exhausted, trembling, and in pain. She muttered thanks, but beyond that could not utter a word.

June found that she now had to pull against the current. She was tired already and soon realized it was impossible. But help was not far off. Some early morning swimmers in the pool had spotted the boat, and one bright fourth-former had fetched a pair of binoculars. As soon as it was seen that the boat was in difficulties, old Tom was sent for – and now here was his small outboard motor-boat chugging along to rescue the two exhausted girls!

They were soon on shore. Matron had been fetched, as soon as June had been recognized through the glasses. No one had spotted Amanda at first, as she was in the bottom of the boat. The girls crowded round, and cried out in horror.

'Oh, look at Amanda's leg and her poor arm! Oh, isn't it *terrible*!'

21 Amanda makes plans

Again the news flew round the school like wild-fire! 'Amanda went swimming out to sea and got caught in the current! June went down to swim in the pool and saw her. She got the little boat and rescued her – but Amanda's badly hurt.'

'Fancy *June* rescuing her bitter enemy!' said the lower-formers. 'Good old June! She's collapsed, Matron says. They are both in the san.'

June soon recovered. She had been completely exhausted, and that and the panic she had felt had knocked her out for a few hours. Then she suddenly sat up and announced that she felt quite all right, could she get up, please?

'Not yet,' said Matron. 'Lie down. I don't want to speak severely to such a brilliant life-saver, but I might, if you don't do what you're told! You certainly saved Amanda's life.'

'How *is* Amanda?' asked June, shivering as she remembered Amanda's terrible leg and arm – bruised and swollen and cut.

'She's not too good,' said Matron. 'Her arm isn't so bad – but the muscles of the leg have been terribly torn. On a rock, I suppose.'

June lay silent. 'Matron – will it – will this mean Amanda can't swim or play games any more this term?'

'It may mean more than that,' said Matron. 'It may mean the end of all swimming and games for her – unless those muscles do their job and heal up marvellously.'

'But – Amanda was going in for the Olympic Games next year,' said June. 'She was good enough, too, Matron.'

'I know all that,' said Matron. 'It's a bad thing this, June. When a person has been given strength and health and a wonderful gift for games, and throws it all away for an hour's forbidden pleasure, it's a tragedy. What that poor girl is thinking of, lying there, I don't like to imagine.'

June didn't like to imagine it, either. How terrible for

Amanda! And to think she had brought it on herself too – that must be even more terrible.

'Can I go and see Amanda?' she asked Matron, suddenly.

'Not today,' said Matron. 'And let me tell you this, June – I know about your clash with Amanda, and I don't care who's right or who's wrong. That girl will want a bit of help and sympathy, so don't you go and see her if you can't be generous enough to give her a bit. You saved her life – that's a great thing. Now you can do a *little* thing, and make it up with her.'

'I'm going to,' said June. 'You're an awful preacher, Matron. I can't imagine why I like you.'

'The feeling is mutual!' said Matron. 'Now, will you please lie down properly?'

June found herself a heroine when she at last got up and went back to school! There were cheers as she came rather awkwardly into the common-room, suddenly feeling unaccountably shy. Susan clapped her on the back, Felicity pumped her right arm up and down, Nora pumped her left.

'Good old June!' chanted the girls. 'Good – old – JUNE!'

'Do shut up,' said June. 'What's the news? I feel as if I've been away for ages. Played any tricks up in the sixth form yet?'

'Good gracious, no! We've been thinking and talking of nothing else but you and Amanda!' said Felicity. 'We haven't once thought of tricks. But we ought to now – just to celebrate your bravery!'

'I wish you wouldn't be an ass,' said June. 'I happened to be there, and saw Amanda in difficulties, that's all. It might have been anyone else.'

But the second-formers would not hide their pride in June. Alicia was pleased and proud too. She came down to clap her small cousin on the back.

'Good work, June,' she said. 'But – it's jolly bad luck on Amanda, isn't it? Out of all games for the rest of the term – and maybe no chance for the Olympic Games next year either.'

No one said, or even thought, that it served Amanda right for her conceit, and for her continual boasting of her prowess. Not even the lower-formers said it, though none of them had liked Amanda. Her misfortune roused their pity. Perhaps the only person in the school who came nearest to thinking that it served Amanda right was the French girl, Suzanne, who had detested Amanda for her brusque ways, and for her contempt of Suzanne herself.

But then Suzanne could not possibly understand *why* Amanda had gone for that long swim, nor could she understand the bitter disappointment of being out of all games for so long.

June was as good as her word. She went to see Amanda as soon as she was allowed to, taking with her a big box of crystallized ginger.

'Hallo, Amanda,' she said, 'how's things?'

'Hallo, June,' said Amanda, who looked pale and exhausted still. 'Oh, I say – thanks for the ginger.'

Matron went out of the room. Amanda turned to June quickly. 'June – I'm not much good at thanking people – but thanks for all you did. I'll never forget it.'

'Now *I'll* say something,' said June. 'And I'll say it for the two of us and then we won't mention it again. We were both idiots over the coaching, *both* of us. I wish the row hadn't happened, but it did. It was fifty-fifty, really. Let's forget it.'

'You might have been in both the second teams,' said Amanda, regretfully.

'I'm going to be!' said June. 'I mean to be! I'm going to practise like anything again – and will you believe it, Moira's offered to time me at swimming each day, and stand and serve me balls at tennis each afternoon!'

Amanda brightened at once. 'That's good,' she said. 'June – I shan't mind things quite so much – being out of everything, I mean – if you *will* get into the second teams. I shan't feel I'm completely wasted then.'

'Right,' said June. 'I'll do my best.'

'And there's another thing,' said Amanda. 'I'm going to spend my time coaching the lower-formers when I'm allowed up. I am to have my leg in plaster and then I can hobble about. I shan't be able to play games myself, but I shall at least be able to see that others play them well.'

'Right,' said June again. 'I'll pick out a few winners for you, Amanda, so that they'll be ready for you when you get up!'

'Time to go, June,' said Matron, bustling in again. 'You'll tire Amanda with all your gabble. But, dear me – she looks much brighter! You'd better come again, June.'

'I'm going to,' said June, departing with a grin. 'Don't eat all Amanda's ginger, Matron. I know your little ways!'

'Well, of all the cheeky young scamps!' said Matron, laughing. But June had gone.

Matron was pleased to see Amanda looking so much brighter. 'June's just like Alicia, that wicked cousin of hers,' she said. 'Yes, and Alicia is just like her mother. I had her mother here, too, when *she* was a girl. Dear,

dear, I must be getting old. The tricks Alicia's mother used to play too. It's a wonder my hair isn't snow-white!'

She left Amanda for an afternoon sleep. But Amanda didn't sleep. She lay thinking. What long long thoughts come to those in bed, ill and in pain! Amanda sorted a lot of things out, during the time she was ill.

Nobody pointed out to her that pride always comes before a fall, but she pointed it out a hundred times to herself. Nobody pointed out that when you had fallen, what really mattered was not the fall, but the getting up again and going on. Amanda meant to get up again and go on. She meant to make up for many many things.

And if my leg muscles never get strong enough for me to play games really well again, I shan't moan and groan, she thought. After all, it's courage that matters, not the things that happen to you. It doesn't really matter *what* happens, so long as you've got plenty of pluck to face it. Courage. Pluck. Well, I *have* got those. I'll be a games mistress if I can't go in for games myself. I like coaching and I'm good at it. It will be second-best but I'm lucky to *have* a second-best.

And so, when she got up and hobbled around, Amanda was welcomed everywhere by the lower-formers, all anxious to shine in her eyes, and to show her that they were sorry for her having to limp about. Amanda marvelled at their short memories. They've forgotten already that I never bothered to help anyone but June, she thought. She gave all her extra time to the eager youngsters, the time that normally she would have had for playing games herself, if it hadn't been for her leg.

'She's really a born games teacher!' the games-mistress said to Miss Peters. 'And now she's taken June on again, and June is so remarkably docile, that kid will be in the second teams in no time!'

So she was, of course, unanimously voted there by Moira, Sally and Darrell. Amanda felt a prick of pride – but a different kind of pride from the kind she had felt before. This time it was a pride in someone else, not in herself.

'And now, my girl,' said Alicia to June, '*now* you can show the stuff you're made of! We had hoped that Amanda might win us all the inter-school shields and cups that there *are* – but she's out of it. So perhaps *you'll* oblige, and really get somewhere for a change!'

22 A most successful trick

The next thing that happened was a good deal pleasanter. The Higher Certificate girls had sat for their exam and at last had got it behind them. They had gone about looking harassed and pale, but made a miraculous recovery immediately the last exam was over.

'And now,' said Alicia, 'I feel I want a bit of relaxation. I want to be silly and laugh till my sides crack! What wouldn't I give to be a second-former just now, and play a few mad tricks on somebody.'

And then the tricks had happened. They were, of

course, planned by the irrepressible second-formers, particularly June and Felicity, who had both been sorry for Darrell and Alicia during their hard exam week.

These two had put their heads together, and had produced a series of exceedingly well-planned tricks. They told the other second-formers, who giggled helplessly.

'These tricks all depend on perfect timing,' said June. 'One we already know – the hair-pin trick – the other is one I've sent for, that I saw advertised in my latest trick booklet.' June had a perfect library of these, and although they were always being confiscated, they were also being continually added to by the indefatigable June.

'We didn't think the hair-pin trick was quite played out, yet,' said Felicity. 'It still has possibilities. But we thought we'd combine it with another trick, which will amaze the sixth-formers as well as Mam'zelle.'

'Good, good, good!' said the eager listeners. 'What is it?'

June explained lucidly. 'Well, listen. See these pellets? They are perfectly ordinary pellets till they're wetted – and then, exactly a quarter of an hour after they're wetted, they swell up into a kind of snake-thing – and they hiss!'

'Hiss?' said Nora, her eyes gleaming. 'What do you mean – hiss?'

'Well, don't you know what "hiss" means?' said June. 'Like this!' And she hissed so violently at Nora that she shrank back in alarm.

'But how *can* they hiss?' she asked.

'I don't know. It's just part of the trick,' said June, impatiently. 'They're wetted – they swell up into funny white snakes – and as they swell, they hiss. In fact, they make a remarkably loud hissing noise! I've got one wetted ready on that desk, so that you can see it working in a few minutes.'

'Oooh,' said the second-formers, in delight.

June went on: 'What I propose to do is to send one of us into the sixth form when Mam'zelle is taking it, and withdraw her hair-pins with the magnet,' said June. 'She'll miss them and rush out to do her hair again. In the meantime, up the chimney there will be one of these pellets, ready wetted – and by it will be a tiny pin-cushion. But instead of pins, it will have hair-pins – just like Mam'zelle's – stuck into it!'

'I see the trick, I see it!' said Katherine, her eyes dancing. 'By the time Mam'zelle has come back and is settled down, the pellet-snake will come out, and began to hiss like anything – and everyone will hear it . . .'

'Yes,' said Felicity, 'and when they go to hunt for the hissing noise, just up the chimney they will find – the little cushion stuck full of Mam'zelle's hair-pins!'

'But won't they see the snake?' asked Nora.

'No – because it falls into the finest powder when it's finished,' said June. 'It can't even be seen. That's the beauty of it. They'll take down the cushion, and won't they gape! I can see my cousin Alicia wondering what it's all about!'

'That's not all,' said Felicity. 'There's still some more. One of us goes into the room again and takes out Mam'zelle's *second* lot of hair-pins – she'll have done her hair again you see – and we'll slip another wetted pellet just behind the blackboard ledge – with another little cushion of hair-pins!'

The second-formers shrieked at this. Oh, to be up in the sixth form when all this happened!

'And the snake will come out, hidden behind the blackboard, on the ledge, and will hiss like fury,' said June. 'And when the hissing is tracked there, they'll find a hair-pin cushion *again*!'

'Priceless,' said Harriet.

'Smashing!' said Nora.

'It's really quite ingenious,' said June, modestly. 'Felicity and I thought it out together. Anyway it will be a real treat for the poor old jaded sixth form, after their week of exams.'

They found out when Mam'zelle was taking a French lesson in the afternoon again. It had to be a time when the second-formers were free, or could go swimming or play tennis. It would be easy to arrange to slip up at the correct times then.

'Wednesday, a quarter to three,' reported June, after examining the time-tables of her form and the sixth. 'Couldn't be better. Nora, you can go in first with the magnet. And, Felicity, you're going in next, aren't you?'

'*I'll* go in first,' said Felicity. 'Who will wet the pellet and put it up the chimney before the class begins?'

'I will,' said June. So, when Wednesday afternoon came, there was much excitement and giggling among the second-formers. Miss Parker wondered what they were up to now. But it was so hot that she really couldn't bother to find out.

June disappeared upstairs just before a quarter to three with the wetted pellet and the little cushion of pins. There was a tiny shelf a little way up the chimney and she carefully placed the pellet at the back and the cushion just in front. Then she fled.

The class filed in a few minutes later. Mam'zelle

arrived. Then Felicity entered, panting. 'Oh please, Mam'zelle, here is a note for you,' she said, and put the envelope down in front of Mam'zelle. The name on it had been written by June, in disguised handwriting. It said 'Mam'zelle Rougier'.

'Why, Felicity, my child, do you not know by now that my name is Mam'zelle Dupont, not Rougier?' said Mam'zelle. 'This is for the other Mam'zelle. Take it to her in the fifth form.'

Felicity was a little behind Mam'zelle. The class looked at her suspiciously. Why the enormous grin on the second-former's face? They soon saw the magnet being held for a few seconds behind Mam'zelle's head. Then Felicity hid the magnet – and its hair-pins – in her hand, took the note, and departed hurriedly.

It was done so quickly that the sixth form gaped. Mam'zelle sensed almost immediately that something was wrong with her hair. She put up her hand, and gave a wail.

'*Oh là là*! Here is my hair undone again!'

And once again she searched in vain for her hair-pins. Knowing from her experience the first time that she would probably not find a single one, she left the room to do her hair, puzzled and bewildered. What was the matter with her hair these days – and her pins too? Mam'zelle seriously considered whether or not it would be advisable to have her hair cut short!

She rushed into her room, did her hair again and stuffed her bun with hair-pins, driving them in viciously as if to dare them to come out! Then she rushed back to the class, patting her bun cautiously.

The hissing began just as she sat down. Up the

chimney the wetted pellet was evolving into a sort of snake, and giving out a loud and insistent hissing noise.

'Ssss-ssss-SSSSSSSS-sss!'

The sixth-formers lifted their heads. 'What is this noise?' asked Mam'zelle, impatiently. 'Alicia, is it you that heesses?'

'No, I don't heess,' said Alicia, with a grin. 'It's probably some noise outside, Mam'zelle.'

'It isn't,' said Moira. 'It's in this room. I'm sure it is.'

The hissing grew louder. 'SSSSSSSSSSSSS!'

'It sounds like a snake somewhere,' said Darrell. 'They hiss just like that. I hope it's not an adder!'

Mam'zelle sprang up with a scream. 'A snake. No, no. There could not be a snake in here.'

'Well, what on earth is it then?' said Sally, puzzled. They all listened in silence.

'SSSSS-sssss-sss-SSS,' said the pellet, loudly and insistently, as the chemicals inside it worked vigorously, pushing out the curious snake-like formation.

Alicia got up. 'I'm going to track it down,' she said. 'It's somewhere near the fireplace.'

She went down on hands and knees and listened. 'It's up the chimney!' she exclaimed in surprise. 'I'll put my hand up and see what's there.'

'No, no, Alicia! Do not do that!' almost squealed Mam'zelle, in horror. 'There is a snake!'

But Alicia was groping up the chimney, pretty certain there was no snake. Her hand closed on something and she pulled it down the chimney.

'Good gracious!' she said, in an astounded voice. 'Look here – your hair-pins, Mam'zelle – in a cushion for you!'

The sixth-formers couldn't believe their eyes. How could Mam'zelle's hair-pins appear miraculously up the chimney, when nobody had gone near the chimney to put them there? And what had made the hissing noise?

'Anyone got a torch?' said Alicia. 'Hallo – the hissing has stopped.'

So it had. The pellet was exhausted. The snake had fallen into the finest of fine powder. When Alicia switched on the torch and shone it up on the little chimney-shelf, there was absolutely nothing to be seen.

Mam'zelle was very angry. She raged and stormed. '*Ah, non, non, non*!' she cried. 'It is not good of you, Alicia, this! Are you not the sixth form? *C'est abominable*! What behaviour! First you take all my hair-pins, then you put them in a cushion, then you hide them up the chimney, and you HEEEEESS!'

'We didn't hiss, Mam'zelle,' protested Darrell. 'It wasn't us hissing. And how *could* we do all that without you seeing us?'

But Mam'zelle evidently thought they were quite capable of doing such miraculous things, and was perfectly certain Alicia or someone had played her a most complicated trick. She snatched at the pin-cushion and threw it violently into the waste-paper basket.

'Abominable!' she raged. 'ABOMINABLE!'

The door opened in the middle of all this and in came Nora, looking as if she could hardly control herself. She was just in time to hear Mam'zelle's yells and see her fling the pin-cushion into the basket. She almost exploded with joy and delight. So the trick had worked!

'Oh, excuse me, Mam'zelle,' she said, politely, smiling at the excited French mistress, 'but have you got

155

a book of Miss Parker's in your desk?'

Mam'zelle was a little soothed by the sight of one of her favourites. She patted her bun to see if it was still there, plus its hair-pins, and tried to control herself. 'Wait now – I will see,' she said, and opened the desk. As June had carefully put a book of Miss Parker's there, in readiness, she had no difficulty in finding it.

And Nora, of course, had no difficulty in holding the magnet close to Mam'zelle's unfortunate bun! The sixth form saw what she was doing and gasped audibly. The cheek! Twice in one lesson! And had the hissing and the cushion been all part of the same trick? Alicia's mind began to work furiously. How had they done it, the clever little monkeys?

Nora had plenty of time to slip the little wetted pellet on the ledge that held the blackboard against the wall, and to place the tiny pin-cushion in front of it, well hidden behind the board. She managed to do this without being seen, as the lid of the desk hid her for a moment, when Mam'zelle opened it to look inside.

Nora took the book thankfully and fled, bursting into gulps and snorts of laughter as she staggered down the corridor. Miss Potts met her and regarded her with suspicion. *Now* what had Nora been up to?

Nora had hardly shut the door when a familiar sensation came over Mam'zelle's head – her hair was coming down. Her bun was uncoiling! In horror she put up her hand and wailed aloud.

'Here it is again – my pins are vanished and gone – my bun, he descends!'

The girls dissolved into laughter. Mam'zelle's face of horror was too comical for words. Suzanne laughed so much that she fell off her chair to the floor. Mam'zelle rose in wrath.

'You! Suzanne! Why do you laugh so? Is it you who have played this treek?'

'*Non*, Mam'zelle, *non*! I laugh only because it is so piggy-hoo-leeEEEARR!' almost wept Suzanne.

Mam'zelle was about to send Suzanne out of the room, when she stopped. The hissing had begun again! There it was. 'Ssssssssssss-ssss!'

'This is too much,' said Mam'zelle, distracted, trying in vain to pin her bun up without any pins. 'It is that snake again. Alicia, look up the chimney.'

'It's not coming from the chimney this time,' said Alicia, puzzled. 'Listen, Mam'zelle. I'm sure it's not.'

They all listened. 'SSSSSSSSSSS!' went the noise merrily. The girls looked at one another. Really, the second-formers were jolly clever – but how *dared* they do all this? Darrell and Alicia grimly made up their minds to have quite a lot to say to Felicity and June after this.

'Ssss-SSSS-sss!'

'It's coming from behind you, Mam'zelle, I'm sure it is,' cried Moira, suddenly. Mam'zelle gave an anguished shriek and propelled herself forward so violently that she fell over the waste-paper basket. She quite thought a snake was coming at her from behind.

Alicia shot out of her seat and went to Mam'zelle's desk, while Darrell and Sally helped Mam'zelle up. 'It's somewhere here,' muttered Alicia, hunting. 'What *can* it be that hisses like that?'

She tracked the noise to the ledge that held the blackboard. Cautiously she put her hand behind – and

157

drew out another little cushion full of pins! The sixth form gaped again! Mam'zelle sank down on a chair and moaned.

'There are my pins once more,' she said. 'But who took them from my bun, who put them in that cushion? There is some invisible person in the room. Ahhhhhhh!'

There was nothing to be seen behind the blackboard at all. Once more the snake had dissolved into fine powder, and the hissing had stopped. The girls began to laugh helplessly again. Moira hissed just behind Mam'zelle and poor Mam'zelle leaped up as if she had been shot. Suzanne promptly fell off her chair again with laughing.

The door opened and everyone jumped. Miss Potts walked in. 'Is everything all right?' she inquired, puzzled at the scene that met her eyes. 'Such peculiar noises came from here as I passed.'

Suzanne got up from the floor. The others stopped laughing. Alicia put the pin-cushion down on the desk. Mam'zelle sat down once more, trying to put up her hair.

'You don't mean to say you've lost your hair-pins *again*, Mam'zelle!' said Miss Potts. 'Your hair's all down.'

Mam'zelle found her voice. She poured out an excited tirade about snakes filling the corners of the room and hissing at her, about cushions appearing full of pins, about hair-pins vanishing from her hair, and then returned to the snakes once more, and began all over again.

'You come with me, Mam'zelle,' said Miss Potts soothingly. 'I'll come back and deal with this. Come along. You shall put your hair up again and you'll feel better.'

'I go to have it cut off,' said Mam'zelle. 'I go now, Miss Potts. This very instant. I tell you, Miss Potts . . .'

But what else she told Miss Potts the sixth-formers didn't know. They sank down on their chairs and laughed again. Those wicked second-formers! Even Alicia had to admit that they had done a very, very clever job!

23 A black day for Gwen

Nobody ticked off the second-formers after all. The sixth agreed that they had had such a wonderful laugh that afternoon that it wasn't really fair to row them. 'It was just what I needed, after that nightmare week of exams,' said Darrell. 'Poor Mam'zelle. She's recovered now, but those wicked little second-formers hiss whenever they walk behind her – and she runs like a hare.'

'They're worse than we ever were,' said Alicia. 'And I shouldn't have thought that was possible!'

Now the term began to slide by very quickly indeed. Darrell could hardly catch at the days as they went by. Matches were played and won. Swimming tournaments were held – and won! Moria, Sally and Darrell played brilliantly and swam well – but the star was June, of course. She was in the second teams for swimming and tennis, the youngest that had ever played in them or swum.

Amanda, still hobbling about, was very proud of June. 'You see! I picked her out, and I told you she was the most promising girl in the school!' she said, exultantly, to the sixth-formers. 'She'll pay for watching and training, that child. She's marvellous!'

Sally and Darrell looked across at one another. What a different Amanda this was now. It had been decided that as she couldn't possibly be allowed to train for any games or sports for at least a year, she should stay on at Malory Towers. And now that Amanda could no longer centre her attention on her own skill and prowess she was centring it on June, and other promising youngsters. Already she had made a great difference to the standard of games among them.

'I shall be able to keep an eye on June, and on one or two others,' went on Amanda, happily. 'I'm sorry you're all leaving, though. It'll be strange without you. Won't you be sorry to go?'

'Gwen's the only one who will be glad to leave Malory Towers,' said Darrell. 'None of the others will – even though we've got college to go to – and Belinda's going to a school of art, and Irene to the Guildhall.'

'And Bill and I to our riding school,' said Clarissa, 'and Moira . . .'

'Oh dear,' said Darrell, interrupting. 'Let's not talk about next term yet. Let's have our last week or two still thinking we're coming back next term. We've had a lot of ups and downs this term – now let's enjoy ourselves.'

They all did – except for one girl. That was Gwen. A black afternoon came for her, one she never forgot. It came right out of the blue, when she least expected it.

Matron came to find her in the common-room. 'Gwen,' she said, in rather a grave voice, 'will you go to Miss Grayling's room? There is someone there to see you.'

Gwen was startled. Who would come and see her so near the end of term? She went down at once. She was amazed to see Miss Winter, her old governess, sitting timidly on a chair opposite Miss Grayling.

'Why – Miss Winter!' said Gwen, astonished. Miss Winter got up and kissed her.

'Oh, Gwen,' she said, 'oh, Gwen!' and immediately burst into tears. Gwen looked at her in alarm.

Miss Grayling spoke. 'Gwen. Miss Winter brings bad news, I'm afraid. She . . .'

'Gwen, it's your father!' said Miss Winter, dabbing her eyes. 'He's been taken dreadfully ill. He's gone to hospital. Oh, Gwen, your mother told me this morning, that he won't live!'

Gwen felt as if somebody had taken her heart right out of her body. She sat down blindly on a chair and stared at Miss Winter.

'Have you – have you come to fetch me to see him?' she said, with an effort. 'Shall I be – in time?'

'Oh, you can't see him,' wept Miss Winter. 'He is much, much too ill. He wouldn't know you. I've come to fetch you home to your mother. She's in such a state, Gwen. I can't do anything with her, not a thing! Can you pack and come right away?'

This was a terrible shock to Gwen – her father ill – her mother desperate – and she herself to leave in a hurry. Then another thought came to her and she groaned.

This would mean no school in Switzerland. In a moment her whole future loomed up before her, not bright and shining with happiness in a delightful new school, but black and full of endless, wearisome jobs for a hysterical mother, full of comfortings for a complaining woman – and with no steady, kindly father in the background.

When she thought of her father Gwen covered her eyes in shame and remorse. 'I never even said good-bye!' she cried out loudly, startling Miss Winter and Miss Grayling. 'I never – even – said – good-bye! And I didn't write when I knew he was ill. Now it's too late.'

Too late! What dreadful words. Too late to say she was sorry, too late to be loving, too late to be good and kind.

'I said cruel things, I hurt him – oh, Miss Winter, why didn't you stop me?' cried Gwen, her face white and her eyes tearless. Tears had always been so easy to Gwen – but now they wouldn't come. Miss Winter looked back at her, not daring to remind Gwen how she had pleaded with her to show a little kindness and not to force her own way so much.

'Gwen, dear – I'm very sorry about this,' said Miss Grayling's kind voice. 'I think you should go and pack now, because Miss Winter wants to catch the next train back. Your mother needs you and you must go. Gwen – you haven't always been all you should be. Now is your chance to show that there is something more in you than we guess.'

Gwen stumbled out of the room. Miss Winter followed to help her to pack. Miss Grayling sat and thought. Somehow punishment always caught up with people, if they had deserved it, just as happiness sooner or later caught up with people who had earned it. You sowed your own seeds and reaped the fruit you had sowed. If only every girl could learn that, thought Miss Grayling, there wouldn't be nearly so much unhappiness in the world!

Darrell came into the dormy as Gwen was packing. She was crying now, her tears almost blinding her.

'Gwen – what's the matter?' said Darrell.

'Oh, Darrell – my father's terribly ill – he's not going to live,' wept Gwen. 'Oh, Darrell, please forget all the horrible, horrible things I've said this term. If only he'd live and I had the chance to make up to him for the beast I've been, I'd do everything he wanted – take the dullest, miserablest job in the world, and give up everything else. But it's too late!'

Darrell was shocked beyond words. She put her arm round Gwen, not knowing what to say. Miss Winter spoke timidly. 'We really must catch that train, Gwen dear. Is this all you have to pack?'

'I'll pack her trunk and see it's sent on,' said Darrell, glad to be able to offer to do something. 'Just take a few things, Gwen, in your night-case.'

She went with Gwen to the front door, miserable for her. What a dreadful way to leave Malory Towers! Poor Gwen! All her fine hopes and dreams blown away like smoke. And those awful words – too late! How dreadful Gwen must feel when she remembered her unkindness. Miss Grayling saw her off too, and shut the door quietly after the car had gone down the drive.

'Don't be too miserable about it,' she said to Darrell. 'It may be the making of Gwen. Don't let it spoil your last week or two, Darrell dear!'

Darrell gave the surprised Miss Grayling a sudden hug, and then wondered how in the world she dared to do such a thing! She went to tell the news to the others.

It cast a gloom on everyone, of course, though many thought secretly that Gwen deserved it. Gwen had no real friends and never had had. She had grumbled and groaned and wept and boasted her way through her years at Malory Towers, and left only unpleasant memories behind. But Sally, Darrell, Mary-Lou and one or two others tried to think kindly of her, because of her great trouble.

Soon other things came to make the girls forget Gwen. Darrell and Sally won the school tennis match against the old girls. Moira won the singles. Someone had a birthday and her mother sent such a magnificent cake that there was enough for everyone in the school! It was delivered in a special van, and carried in by two people!

Then news came of Jo. It came through Deirdre. She received a parcel from Jo and a letter.

> Here's some things for you I got myself [wrote Jo]. And I've packed them myself too. I don't know what I'm going to do yet. Dad says he won't be able to get me into a school as good as Malory Towers, I'll have to go to any that will take me. But I don't mind telling you I'm not going to be idiotic again. Dad's been a brick, but he's awfully cut up really. He keeps saying it's half his fault. Mother's fed up with me. She shouldn't have kept boasting I was at Malory Towers. She says I've let the family name down. All I can say is, it's a good thing it's only 'Jones'.

I'm sorry I got you into a row, and I'm awfully glad they didn't expel you too. I wish you'd do something for me. I wish you'd tell the second-formers (go to Felicity) that I apologize for not owning up that time. Will you? That's been on my conscience for ages.

I do miss Malory Towers. Now I know I'm not going back again I see how splendid it was.

Hope you like the parcel.

JO

Deirdre took the letter to Felicity, who read it in silence and then handed it back. 'Thanks,' she said. 'I'll tell the others. And – er – give her best wishes from the second-formers, will you? Don't forget. Just that – best wishes from the second-formers.'

News came from Gwen too – news that made Darrell heave a sigh of relief. Gwen's father was not going to die. Gwen had seen him. It hadn't been too late after all. He would be an invalid for the rest of his life, and Gwen would certainly now have to take a job – but she was trying to be good about it.

It's mother who is so difficult [she wrote]. She just cries and cries. Well, I might have grown like that too, if this hadn't happened to me. I shall never be as strong-minded and courageous as you, Darrell – or Sally – or Bill and Clarissa – but I don't think I'll ever again be as weak and selfish as I was. You see – it wasn't 'too late' after all. And that has made a lot of difference to me. I feel as if I've been given another chance.

165

Do, do, do write to me sometimes. I think and think of you all at Malory Towers. I know none of you think of me, but you might just write occasionally.

All the best to the form and you.

GWEN

Darrell did write, of course. She wrote at once. Darrell was happy and had a happy future to look forward to, and she could well afford to spill a little happiness into Gwen's dull and humdrum life. Sally wrote too and so did Mary-Lou. Bill and Clarissa sent photographs of the stables they meant to set up as a riding school in the autumn.

And now indeed the last term was drawing to an end. Tidying up of shelves and cupboards began. Personal belongings from the sixth-form studies were sent home. Trunks were lugged down from the attics. All the familiar bustle of the last days of term began once more. Belinda drew her last 'scowl', and Irene hummed her last tune. The term was almost finished.

24 Last day

'Last day, Darrell,' said Sally, when they awoke on the very last morning. 'And thank goodness it's sunny and bright. I couldn't bear to leave on a rainy day.'

'Our last day!' said Darrell. 'Do you remember the first, Sally – six years ago? We were little shrimps of twelve – smaller than Felicity and June! How the time has flown!'

The last-day bustle began in earnest after breakfast. Matron was about the only calm person in the school, with the exception of Miss Grayling, whom nobody had ever seen flustered or ruffled. Mam'zelle was as usual in a state of beaming, bewildered good temper. Miss Potts bustled about with first-formers who had lost this, that or the other.

The trunks had most of them gone off in advance, but those being taken by car were piled up in the drive. Pop, the handyman, ran about like a hare, and carried heavy trunks on his broad shoulder as if they weighed only a pound or two. The first car arrived and hooted in the drive. An excited third-former squealed and almost fell down the stairs from top to bottom when she recognized her parents' car.

'*Tiens*!' said Mam'zelle, catching her. 'Is this the way to come down the stairs? Always you hurry too much, Hilary!'

'Come down to the pool, Sally,' said Darrell. They went down the steep path and stood beside the gleaming, restless pool, which was swept every now and again by an extra big wave coming over the rocks. 'We've had fun here,' said Darrell. 'Now let's go to the rose-garden.'

They went there and looked at the masses of brilliant roses. Each was silently saying good-bye to the places she loved most. They went to all the common-rooms, from the first to the sixth, remembering what had happened in each. They peeped into the dining-room, and then into the different form-rooms. What fun they had had!

And what fun they were *going* to have! 'We'll have a good look backwards, today, then we'll set our eyes forwards,' said Sally. 'College will be better fun still, Darrell – everyone says so.'

June and Felicity caught sight of the two sixth-formers wandering around. June nudged Felicity. 'Look – they're saying a fond farewell. Don't they look solemn?'

June caught up with the sixth-formers. 'Hallo,' she said. 'You've forgotten something.'

'What?' asked Sally and Darrell.

'You've forgotten to say good-bye to the stables and the wood-shed, and . . .'

'That's not funny,' said Darrell. 'You wait till it's your last day, young June!'

'June's got no feelings at all, have you, June?' said Alicia, appearing round the corner. 'I feel a bit solemn myself today. Here, you two youngsters, this can jolly well be a solemn day for you too!'

To June's intense surprise she took her by the shoulders and looked into her eyes. 'Carry on for me,' she said. 'Carry the standard high! Do you promise, June?'

'I promise,' said June, startled. 'You – you can trust me, Alicia.'

'And I promise, Darrell,' said Felicity, equally solemnly. 'I'll never let Malory Towers down. *I'll* carry the standard high too.'

Alicia released June's shoulders. 'Well,' she said, 'so long as we've got *some*one to hand on the standard to, I'm happy! Maybe our own daughters will help to carry on the tradition one day.'

'And have riding lessons on Bill's and Clarissa's horses,' said Felicity, which made them all laugh.

There was more hooting in the drive. 'Come on. We shan't be ready when our people arrive,' said Alicia. 'That sounds like my brother Sam hooting. He said he'd come and fetch me today.'

Into the seething crowd they went. Mam'zelle was shouting for someone who had gone long since, and Suzanne was trying to explain to her that she wasn't there. Miss Potts was carrying a pair of pyjamas that had apparently dropped out of someone's night-case. Matron rushed after a small first-former anxiously, nobody could imagine why. It was the old familiar last-morning excitement.

'Darrell! Felicity!' suddenly called Mrs. Rivers's voice. 'Here we are! Where on earth were you? We've been here for ages.'

'Oh, that was *Daddy's* horn we heard hooting,' said Felicity. 'I might have guessed. Come on, Darrell. Got your case?'

'Yes, *and* my racket,' said Darrell. 'Where's yours?'

Felicity disappeared into the crowd. Mr. Rivers kissed Darrell and laughed. 'Doing her disappearing act already,' he said.

'Good-bye, Darrell! Don't forget to write!' yelled Alicia. 'See you in October at St Andrews.'

She stepped back heavily on Mam'zelle's foot. 'Oh, sorry, Mam'zelle.'

'Always you tread on my feet,' said Mam'zelle, quite unfairly. 'Have you seen Katherine? She has left her racket behind.'

Felicity ran up with her own racket. 'Good-bye,

Mam'zelle. Be careful of snakes these holidays, won't you?'

'Ahhhhhhh! You bad girl, you,' said Mam'zelle. 'I heeeess at you! Ssssssss!'

This astonished Miss Grayling considerably. She was just nearby, and got the full benefit of Mam'zelle's ferocious hiss. Mam'zelle was covered with confusion and disappeared hurriedly.

Darrell laughed. 'Oh dear – I do love this last-minute flurry. Oh – are we off, Daddy? Good-bye, Miss Grayling, good-bye, Miss Potts, good-bye, Mam'zelle – good-bye, Malory Towers!'

And good-bye to you, Darrell – and good luck. We've loved knowing you. Good-bye!

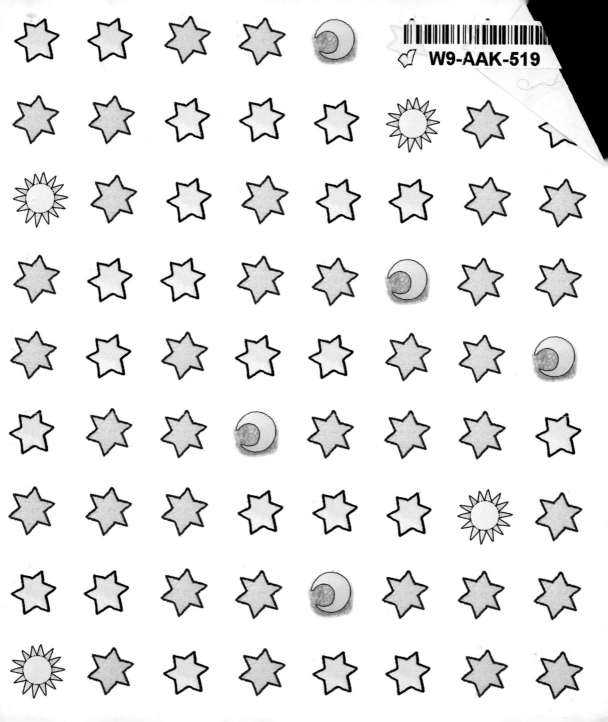

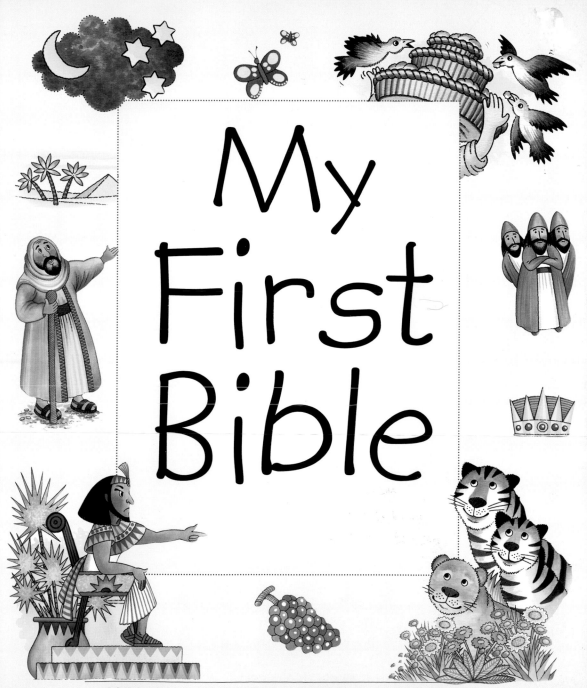

My First Bible

CONCORDIA PUBLISHING HOUSE • SAINT LOUIS

Contents—Old Testament

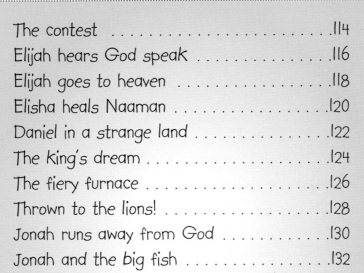

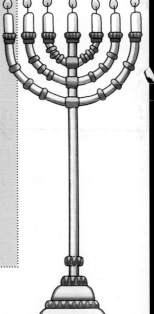

Contents—New Testament

The Old Testament

In the beginning

Genesis 1:1–10, 14–16

A very, very long time ago, at the beginning
of time, God created the world out of
nothing through His Word.

God made the light and the darkness.

God made huge, tall mountains.

God made deep blue seas and oceans.

God made the round earth to spin, the
fiery sun to shine, and the silvery moon
to glow. God made twinkling stars
and mysterious planets.

God made the plants and trees

Genesis 1:11–12

The earth looked brown and bare.

So God made plants and trees to grow on the land. He made tall trees with bark and branches, leaves, berries, and cones. He made small bushes, shrubs, the prickly cactus, and hairy coconuts.

God saw what He had made and thought that it was good.

17

God made the fish and animals

Genesis 1:20–25

God filled the seas and oceans with slippery, shiny fish, spouting whales, and squiggly octopuses.

God filled the sky above with beautiful birds: the great eagle that soared up to the mountain tops, the bright kingfisher that darted near the water.

Their songs filled the land:

tweeting,

cawing,

and trilling.

18

God made animals of every kind:
tall and short, prickly and furry, striped
and spotted
and patterned.
They roamed freely
and ate the lush,
green grass
and plants.

19

Adam and Eve

Genesis 1:26–31; 2:8–15

"Now I will make people," said God.

God created Adam and Eve —
a man and a woman. They could think
and feel and love. God made them
in His image, which means they were
holy like Him. He asked them to look
after the animals.

God made a beautiful place for
them to live in called the Garden of
Eden. God was pleased with everything He had
made. It was
very good.

Adam and Eve sin

Genesis 2:16–17; 3:1–24

God told Adam, "You may eat the fruit from any tree in the garden except from the tree of knowledge of good and evil. If you eat that tree's fruit, you will die."

But the serpent said to Eve, "You won't really die, you know. Have a taste. It's good!"

So Eve took the fruit and had a bite. Then she gave some to Adam. He ate some too. Adam and Eve had broken God's rules.

God was very angry because they sinned and sent them out of the garden of Eden forever. God punished Adam and Eve for disobeying, but He promised to send His people a Savior to take away their sin.

23

Noah and his family

Genesis 6:9–12, 17

Faithful Noah was a good man. He listened and *believed* when God spoke to him.

Noah had a wife and three sons: Shem, Ham, and Japheth.

Sadly, the world was no longer the good place God had made.

Sin brought trouble to the world. People were fighting each other. God was angry. He told Noah what He planned to do. God was going to send a great flood to cover the whole earth because of sin.

Noah builds
the ark

Genesis 6:14–16

God told Noah to
build a huge wooden
boat called an ark:

"Get some good strong wood to build the boat, and cover it inside and out with tar. Put a roof on the top and build rooms inside. Put a door on one side. When the flood comes, you will be safe."

Noah did as God said. People watched and wondered. They even laughed at him! Why was he building a boat so far from the sea?

The animals enter the ark

Genesis 7:1–5

God wanted there to be animals
on the earth after the flood.

So God told Noah to bring
animals, birds, and reptiles into
the ark, male and female of every kind.

"I will send rain for forty days and
nights," said God, "and a great flood
will cover every living thing in the world."

Only Noah, his family, and the animals
would be safe inside the ark.

Storing food

Genesis 6:21–22

God told Noah to store up enough food to feed all the animals in the ark and enough for his own family too. That was a lot of food!

Noah and his sons worked hard to get everything ready.

They collected food from the land and stored it in the ark. When the flood came, there would be no more food to eat until it all grew again, fresh and new.

Here comes the flood!

Genesis 7:11–24

When the ark was ready, Noah and his family went inside. God closed the door.

Water burst up from the ground. Then the rain began to pour down. It rained and it rained, for forty days and nights.

First the water covered the land. Then it covered the trees. Soon even the tallest mountains were hidden by water!

Nothing was left alive on the earth except for Noah and his family and the animals in the ark. God kept them very safe.

33

Inside the ark

Genesis 7:23–24

Inside the ark, they were warm and safe. Noah and his family heard the rain drumming on the roof.

They saw the water all around the ark.

The animals were noisy, especially when it came to feeding time. But there was enough food for everyone.

All they could do now was wait for the rain to stop.

The promise of the rainbow

Genesis 8:4, 15–19; 9:8–17

At long last, the rain stopped. God sent wind to dry the water. Dry land appeared!

The ark came to rest on the mountains of Ararat.

Noah came out of the ark. He praised God for saving his family and keeping them alive.

God put a beautiful rainbow in the sky as a promise that He would never send another flood to cover the whole earth. When we see a rainbow, we can remember that God keeps His promises, especially His promise to save us from our sin through His Son, Jesus.

The tower of Babel

Genesis 11:1–9

When the earth was full of people again, they decided to build a city. They learned how to bake bricks in the sun and stuck them together with tar.

"Let's build a tower that reaches to the sky!" they said. "Everyone will see how important we are."

But God saw what they were planning. He knew they were forgetting about Him.

So God mixed up their languages. They couldn't understand each other anymore! It all sounded like babble.

God scattered the people all over the earth and they stopped building the city.

God's promise to Abraham

Genesis 12:1–2

Abraham was a good man.

God promised that Abraham's children would bless the earth. The problem was, Abraham and his wife Sarah could not have any children.

"Abraham!" said God. "Look at the stars and try to count them. You will have as many people in your family as the number of stars you can see."

Abraham believed God's special promise. He was willing to wait.

Sure enough, when Abraham was ninety-nine years old, God's promise came true. Abraham and Sarah had a baby boy.

Abraham and Sarah were so happy that they named their son "Isaac," which means "laughter." Abraham and Isaac were Jesus' ancestors.

Rebekah's kindness

Genesis 24:1–61

Rebekah was a beautiful girl. She
was also very kind. Every day
she fetched water from the well
for her family.

One afternoon, she noticed a
man standing at the well with
his ten camels.

Rebekah offered a drink of
water to the man and his camels.
God had told the man that this
would be a sign that this was
the girl to be Isaac's wife.

Then the man took a beautiful gold ring and gold bracelets out of his bag and put them on Rebekah. She had never seen anything so fine!

"Take me to your father's house," he said.

So they set off to see Rebekah's family. The man said that he had come to find a wife for Abraham's son, Isaac. He asked if Rebekah would be Isaac's wife. She agreed and set off the next day to marry Isaac.

43

Isaac and Rebekah have twins

Genesis 25:19–28

Isaac and Rebekah were very happy together.

After a few years, they had twin boys called Esau and Jacob.

Although they were twins, the boys were very different.

Esau had red hair and he was hairy all over. He loved hunting and being outdoors with his bow and arrows.

Jacob had smooth skin. He loved being at home.

44

He was a good cook and made wonderful soups and stews for his family.

Esau was born first. This meant that when Isaac, their father, died, Esau would be given all that his father owned and a special blessing.

Jacob secretly wanted to be the one to get the blessing and all that his father had, so he planned a nasty trick.

Jacob and Esau

Genesis 25:29–34; 27:1–45

One day, Esau came home from hunting and was very hungry. He could smell some delicious soup Jacob was cooking.

"Give me that soup!" said Esau.

"Only if you promise to let me get everything from Dad as if I was the eldest," said Jacob.

Esau cared only about his hungry tummy.

"Oh, all right," he said. "Just let me have that soup!"

Esau got the soup and Jacob got their father's possessions and blessing.

A few years later, Jacob tricked their father, too, when he was dying.

He dressed up in goat's skin so his skin would feel hairy, like his brother's. Their old father could not see well and thought it was Esau. So he gave Jacob the special blessing. Esau was furious when he found out.

Jacob ran away from home. It was years later that he came back and said he was sorry to Esau for the nasty tricks he had played.

Joseph and his brothers

Genesis 35:23–26

Abraham believed that God would keep His promise and give him a big family.

And God kept His promise.

Abraham's grandson, Jacob, had a very large family. He had twelve sons and a daughter. He lived with his family in the land of Canaan.

Jacob's sons looked after his sheep and goats.

Jacob's sons were called Reuben, Simeon, Levi, Judah, Issachar, Zebulun, Dan, Naphtali, Gad, Asher, Joseph, and Benjamin.

Of all his sons, Jacob loved Joseph the most. Joseph was Jacob's favorite son.

Joseph's new coat

Genesis 37:3–4

When Joseph was seventeen years old,
his father, Jacob, gave him a very special
present. He gave him a wonderful new coat
to wear.

Joseph was very proud of his new coat.
He strutted around in front of all his
brothers, saying, "Look at me! Look what
Dad has bought for me!"

But Joseph's brothers were jealous.

"Why does Dad love Joseph more than
us?" they muttered.

"Why haven't we been given coats like
that?" they grumbled.

Joseph didn't seem to hear them.
He thought only about his coat.

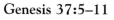

Joseph's dreams

Genesis 37:5–11

One night, Joseph had a very strange dream. He dreamed there were eleven sheaves of grain, that all bowed down to his sheaf.

Then he dreamed he saw eleven stars, the sun and the moon, all bowing down to him!

Joseph told his family all about his dreams. But it made his brothers very angry.

"Why does Joseph think he is more important than us?" they asked.

"Do you think you are going to be a king and rule over us, Joseph?" they mocked.

Joseph's brothers were very jealous.

Joseph is sold as a slave

Genesis 37:12–35

One day when all the brothers were in
the fields looking after the sheep, they
thought up a cruel plan to get rid of Joseph.
They had heard enough of his stories about
grain and stars bowing to him!

When Joseph came to see them, they
threw him into an empty well. They were
planning to leave him there to die, but
then a group of travelling traders
came past. They were on their
way to Egypt. The brothers quickly
changed their plan and
sold Joseph to the
traders.

54

He was taken away as a slave!

The brothers told their father that Joseph had been killed by a wild animal. They thought they would never see Joseph again.

But God had other plans for Joseph.

Joseph understands dreams

Genesis 39:1–40:23

Joseph worked hard in Egypt for his new master, Potiphar, the captain of the guard. But Potiphar's wife told lies about Joseph and he ended up in jail!

In jail, Joseph met the King's chief baker and the King's wine steward. One night they both had very strange dreams. Joseph understood the dreams.

The wine steward spoke first: "I saw a grapevine with three branches. The grapes became ripe and I squeezed them into the King's cup and gave it to him to drink."

Joseph told him happily that in three days he would be freed from jail.

The baker spoke next, but his dream did not end so happily.

"I was carrying three baskets of cakes and pastries, when some birds swooped down and ate them all up!" said the baker.

Joseph looked very sad, and said, "I'm sorry to say, you will never be free. The king means to kill you in three days!"

Three days later, the dreams came true, just as Joseph had said!

Joseph helps Pharaoh

Genesis 41:1–41

Two years later, the King of Egypt began to have strange dreams that no one could understand. The wine steward, whom Joseph had helped in jail, remembered Joseph and told the King all about him.

Joseph was brought before the great king of Egypt.

"Your majesty, tell me your dreams," said Joseph.

"I was standing on the river bank when seven fat cows came out of the river to feed," said the King. "Then seven thin cows came and ate them all up.

But they stayed as thin as before. Then I dreamed I saw seven fat ears of corn, which were then eaten up by seven thin ears of corn. What does this mean?"

Joseph told the King that there would be a time of great famine in the land. He must store up food for seven years to feed the people because there would be no food for the seven years after that.

The King was pleased with what Joseph said and put him in charge of storing food for Egypt.

Together again

Genesis 42:1–8; 45; 46:1–7

One day, Joseph's brothers came to Egypt to ask for food. There was none left in Canaan.

They did not recognize their brother Joseph. Many years had passed and Joseph was older now.

They begged for food to take home to their father in Canaan.

When Joseph told them who he really was, they cried and said they were sorry for what they had done to him all those years before.

Once again, the family was back together. Joseph's father, Jacob, came to Egypt to live until the end of his days.

The baby in the basket

Exodus 1:22–2:10

Moses was born in Egypt at a time when there was a cruel king. The king turned God's people into slaves. The king was afraid of God's people. He ordered that all their baby boys should be thrown into the Nile river !

One mother tried to save her baby boy. She made a special basket of reeds and painted it with tar so it would float. She placed her son in the basket and hid it

62

in the long bulrushes at the side of the river. The baby's sister, Miriam, hid close by and watched.

A royal princess came to the river to bathe and heard the baby crying. She lifted him out of the basket. She wanted to help the baby.

Miriam stepped out from behind the bulrushes.

"I know who can feed the baby!" she said to the princess.

She fetched her mother. So Moses was looked after by his own mother. When he was old enough, he went to live in the palace with the princess.

63

Moses runs away

Exodus 2:11–15

When Moses grew up, he saw how cruelly his people were treated by the king.

Once he saw an Egyptian beating a slave. Moses was furious. He looked to see if anyone was watching, then he stepped forward and killed the Egyptian.

Moses buried him in the sand.

The next day, Moses saw two slaves fighting and tried to stop them.

One of them said, "Well, are you going to kill me next, like you killed that Egyptian yesterday?"

Moses was very afraid: someone had seen him after all.

Moses ran away, far from the king's palace, to a land called Midian.

The burning bush

Exodus 3:1–10

Moses became a shepherd. One day,
he saw a very strange sight: a bush on
fire. Flames crackled and licked the dry
branches, but the bush did not burn up!
In fact, it was the angel of the Lord!

A voice from inside the bush called:
"Moses! Moses!"

Moses trembled and stepped closer
to the bush. Could it be God speaking?

"Take off your sandals," said God.
"You are standing on holy ground."

Moses covered his eyes.

"I am the God of your father,
the God of Abraham, the God of Isaac,

and the
God of
Jacob,"
said God.
"I have heard
My people's cries
for help. I want you
to go to the cruel
king and bring My
people out of Egypt.
I will give them a
new land of their
own, which will
be full of
good things."

67

The plagues of Egypt

Exodus 7:14–11:8

Moses went to the king, but he would not let the people leave Egypt. So God sent terrible plagues to change the king's mind. The water of the River Nile turned to blood.

Then hundreds of croaking frogs hopped into everyone's houses and beds! Next came gnats and flies, which buzzed into the Egyptians' houses.

68

All the cows and sheep died. Then all the Egyptians were covered in boils and their skin became terribly sore. Still the King wouldn't change his mind.

Hailstones hit the land. Locusts came and devoured the crops. Darkness fell upon the land and no one could see.

But the last plague would be the most terrible of all. Moses warned the King that all the firstborn children of Egypt would die in one night.

The Passover feast

Exodus 12:1–8, 29–32

Moses told God's people to get ready.

"Take a lamb, kill it, and put some of the lamb's blood on the doorposts of the house," he said. "Roast the lamb over a fire and eat the meat with bitter herbs and bread made without yeast. This is the Passover."

That night, death came to Egypt. All the firstborn sons and animals of the Egyptians died. Even the King's son died.

But death passed over all the homes of God's people, and God saved them all.

The King said to Moses, "Go! Leave Egypt! Take your animals and go as you asked."

The King finally decided to let the people go.

70

Moses crosses the Red Sea

Exodus 14:5–31

Moses led God's people away from
Egypt where they had been slaves. But as
they camped for the night near the Red Sea,
they saw the King's chariots and horsemen
charging toward them! The King had changed
his mind again!

But Moses said, "Don't be afraid! God
will help us."

God told Moses to walk toward the Red
Sea with his stick held high.

God moved the water back with a strong
wind and a path of dry ground appeared at
the bottom of the sea.

Moses led his people
across the path to
safety on the other
side of the Red Sea.

The Egyptian army tried to follow
but their chariot wheels got stuck in the
ground. Once again, God told Moses to
hold out his hand over the water. The Red
Sea came crashing back down over the
Egyptian army.

Moses led his people on toward the
new land God had promised to his people.

Food in the desert

Exodus 16:1–18

"We're hungry!" grumbled the people.

God had guided them across the Red Sea to safety on the other side, away from the Egyptian army and the cruel king at last. But now the Israelites were grumbling. And their stomachs were rumbling.

"I will send bread from heaven," said God to Moses. That evening, quail flew over the camp and the people caught them.

In the morning, dew covered the ground. When it had gone, there were flakes of white manna on the ground. It was the bread from heaven that God had sent. It tasted like wafers made with honey.

God had provided all they needed. He sent enough food for them each day.

God gives the
Ten Commandments

Deuteronomy 5:1–22

Moses climbed Mount Sinai to talk to God.

"I am the Lord your God, who rescued you when you were slaves in Egypt," said God. "Obey Me and I will make your nation great," said God.

"Do not pray to or praise any other gods but Me.

"Don't pray to statues, pictures, or things of the earth, sky or sea instead of Me.

"Think about how you use My name; do not swear or use My name carelessly.

76

"Remember the day of rest I give you at the end of the week.

"Love your mother and father and listen to what they say.

"Do not plot to kill anyone.

"Be faithful to your husband or wife.

"Do not steal.

"Do not tell lies about other people.

"Don't look greedily at things that belong to other people."

There was a trumpet blast and the words were written on stone tablets. These laws are called the Ten Commandments.

The tabernacle

Exodus 25:8–40

It took many years to reach the land that God had promised to His people.

On the way there, God spoke to Moses many times. He told Moses to build the tabernacle – a holy place where God was and where people worshiped Him.

The tabernacle was a special tent. Moses' brother, Aaron, was made a high priest. He was the only one who could go into the holiest part of the tabernacle.

Special objects were made for the tabernacle: a golden lampstand and the ark of the covenant. This was a sacred

box that contained the stone tablets with the commandments God gave to Moses on Mount Sinai.

God's tabernacle was a very holy place. People came to say sorry to God for the wrong things they had done and to ask for God's blessing.

Joshua becomes a leader

Deuteronomy 34; Joshua 3

God took Moses to the top of a mountain. From there he could see a new land in the distance. It was the Promised Land!

But Moses never set foot there. He died.

God chose Joshua to lead the people for the rest of the journey. God spoke to Joshua:

"Moses is dead. You and all My people must cross the River Jordan to reach the land I have promised to give to you.

I will be with you, as I always was with Moses. I will never leave you. Be brave."

Joshua ordered the officers of the people to be prepared to cross the river.

The priests went on ahead, carrying the ark of the covenant from the tabernacle. The water stopped flowing and the people crossed the river on dry ground. It was a miracle.

Joshua and the walls of Jericho

Joshua 6:1–21

To reach the Promised Land, God's people had to get past the city of Jericho.

The city had huge, thick stone walls. It seemed impossible to get through. But God had a plan.

God told Joshua to choose seven priests with trumpets made of rams' horns. He said they must march around the city once every day for six days, blowing their trumpets, following the ark of the covenant.

On the seventh day, the priests had to march round six times. Then on the seventh time, the priests sounded a long trumpet blast on their horns, the people shouted and... the mighty walls of Jericho fell to the ground.

God had given them the city of Jericho.

Gideon's victory

Judges 6:11–7:22

Years later, when Joshua died, God's people began to turn away from God and His Commandments. So God sent judges to guide the people. One of the judges was Gideon.

Gideon was chosen to lead the army. He knew that God was on his side and would help him. They had to fight the strong Midianite army.

Gideon gave each soldier a ram's horn trumpet and a jar with a burning torch inside.

"This is what we must do," he said.

"When I reach the edge of the camp, watch carefully and copy me. When I blow my trumpet, blow yours too and shout, 'A sword for the Lord and for Gideon!'"

So Gideon and his men came to the edge of the enemy camp in the middle of the night. They blew their trumpets and broke the jars they were holding. All the other soldiers copied them. They broke their jars, picked up their trumpets, and shouted: "A sword for the Lord and for Gideon!"

The enemy army ran away! God had helped Gideon win the battle.

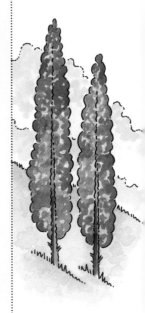

The strength of Samson

Judges 14:5–6; 16:4–30

God had made Samson a very strong man.
He could kill a lion with his bare hands.
Samson had long hair, that was braided in
seven braids. If his hair was ever cut, his
strength would go. But that was a secret.

The Philistines were enemies of God's
people. They wanted to find out the secret
of Samson's strength so they could defeat
him. They paid a woman named Delilah to
find out the secret.

Delilah asked Samson many times.
Finally he told her about his hair.

Delilah told the Philistines, and when Samson was asleep, the Philistines cut off his hair! They captured Samson and threw him into prison.

But Samson's hair started to grow again.

Samson was kept in chains. One day, when the Philistines were meeting in their temple, Samson pushed against the pillars of the temple with all his might.

God gave Samson strength one more time.

The temple fell down with a mighty crash and all the Philistines were crushed beneath the great pillars.

Ruth

Naomi was sad. She had left her home
to find food in another land because there
was none in Israel. Then her husband and her
sons had died. Naomi was all alone except
for Ruth and Orpah, the wives of her sons.

Naomi got ready to travel home. Ruth
was very kind and would not leave Naomi.

"Where you go, I will go," said Ruth.
"Your people will be my people, and your
God will be my God."

Ruth worked hard all day, gathering leftover corn from the edges of the harvest fields. She made bread to feed Naomi and herself.

The farmer of the fields, Boaz, watched Ruth and saw how good and kind she was to Naomi. Before long, Boaz asked Ruth to marry him! They had a baby boy called Obed.

Naomi held her grandson, Obed, lovingly in her arms. She had once been so sad, but now God had given her great happiness.

Samuel
listens to God

1 Samuel 3:1–18

Samuel was a young boy who lived in the Temple. He helped Eli, the priest, look after the lampstand.

One night, after Samuel had gone to bed, he heard a voice calling his name: "Samuel! Samuel!"

Samuel ran to Eli. "Here I am. You called me," he said.

But Eli told him to go back to bed. "I didn't call you!"

Then Samuel heard the voice again.

He ran straight to Eli.

"Here I am!" he said.

"No, I did not call you!" said Eli.

It happened a third time.

Then Eli realized that it must be God calling and said to Samuel, "Next time you hear Him calling, say, 'Here I am, Lord, your servant is listening.'"

Samuel went back to bed and he heard God's voice again.

Samuel did as Eli said and listened carefully to God. God told him many things. In the morning Samuel told Eli all about it.

Samuel was only a young boy, but God had chosen him to be a special messenger.

David the shepherd boy

1 Samuel 16:11–13

David was a shepherd boy. He looked after his father's sheep on the hills. He led them to pastures of green grass. He took them to streams of clear water where they could drink.

If one of the sheep was lost, David would look everywhere for it until he found it.

Sometimes there was danger. Wild animals tried to snatch the sheep and lambs. If a lion or a bear tried to carry off one of the flock, David would kill it. He was very brave.

David played the harp and sang songs to God.

God had a plan for David. He told Samuel to anoint David to be the next king of Israel.

David plays for King Saul

1 Samuel 16:14–23

King Saul became a very troubled man because he had not done what God had told him to do. He often sat in his room feeling terrible. His servants thought it might help him to listen to some music.

"There is a boy in Bethlehem," said one servant, "who is very good at playing the harp. His name is David. He takes care of his father's sheep."

Saul asked them to fetch David. Saul did not know that David had been anointed by Samuel to be the next king.

King Saul listened to David playing the harp and the music helped him to feel calm again.

"Stay here," he said to David. "I wish to hear more."

So David stayed with the king. Whenever the king felt terrible, David would play beautiful music on his harp.

David and Goliath

1 Samuel 17:17–54

Goliath was a real giant in the Philistine army! Nobody in the army dared fight him.

One day, David left his sheep to take food to his brothers, who were soldiers in the camp.

David heard Goliath shouting, "Who will fight me?"

"I will fight him!" said David. "God will help me!"

David went to the river and chose five

smooth stones. He took out his sling, then set off to face Goliath. With a quick flick of his wrist, he whirled the sling round his head and threw one of the stones at Goliath. It hit Goliath on the forehead and killed him!

The Philistines turned and ran away, chased by King Saul's army. Everyone cheered for David, who had bravely killed a giant with the help of God.

David is made king

2 Samuel 5:1–4

The people loved David very much. King Saul was jealous of David, and he tried to kill David, so David hid from him for a long time. He hid in the land of the Philistines because he knew King Saul would not look for him there. The Philistines were King Saul's enemies. They wanted to kill Saul and his sons.

God saw that King Saul no longer obeyed

Him or ruled in a way that honored God.

The Philistines came after King Saul, and Saul and his sons were killed.

David was very sad when he heard the news. He had been good friends with Jonathan, Saul's son. David wept.

But many years before, Samuel had anointed David and now it was time for him to be king.

David was a strong ruler of God's people. He fought bravely against their enemies and people cheered as he rode by on his mighty horse.

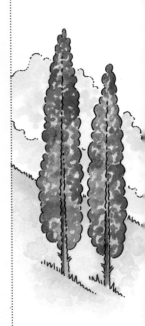

Solomon's wisdom

1 Kings 3:5–9, 16–28

God told King
Solomon to ask
Him for anything
he wanted.

"Please help
me to know what
is right and wrong,"
said Solomon.

A while later,
two women came
to see King Solomon.
They were fighting
over a baby.

Each woman said she was the baby's mother. Solomon thought of a way to find out the truth.

"Fetch a sword," he said, "and cut the baby in half."

"Yes," said one woman. "Then at least we'll both get something."

"No!" shouted the other. "You mustn't hurt the baby. The other woman can keep him."

King Solomon knew at once that the real mother didn't want her baby to be hurt. Solomon gave her back the baby.

God had helped Solomon to decide wisely.

King Solomon builds the Temple 1 Kings 6

King David's son Solomon became king after his father. He loved God and wanted to build a magnificent temple in Jerusalem. This would be a special place where God would be present and people would worship Him.

Solomon ordered thirty thousand men from all over Israel to chop down cedar trees in Lebanon and bring the wood back for the Temple. Then thousands of men prepared the wood and stone. It would be the most magnificent building Israel had ever seen.

The inside of the Temple was lined with panels of cedar wood. Within the Temple Solomon prepared the Most Holy Place. The ark of the covenant would be kept there. Solomon had the inside of the Most Holy Place and the inside of the Temple covered with pure gold. He had huge angels made of olive wood to guard the inner room.

It took Solomon seven years to build the Temple. There had never been a finer building in Jerusalem.

Elijah and King Ahab

1 Kings 17:1

Elijah was a prophet. God often spoke to him and Elijah listened. God told him to give messages to the people of Israel.

At this time Israel was ruled by King Ahab. There had been many kings of Israel since King Solomon, some good and some bad.

Ahab was one of the bad kings.

God gave Elijah a message for the king. Elijah knew he must go to King Ahab and speak firmly.

"Ahab!" said Elijah. "There is going to be a terrible drought. There will be no rain for many years. It will come only when God gives the word."

107

Elijah and the ravens

1 Kings 17:2–7

Elijah was in great danger.

King Ahab and his wife didn't like what God's prophets were saying so they were trying to kill them.

God told Elijah to hurry to the east of the land and hide in the Kerith Ravine. God said He would provide everything Elijah needed.

"I have ordered ravens to feed you," said God.

108

Sure enough,
ravens brought
Elijah bread and
meat every
morning and
evening. Elijah
drank the cool water
from the brook in the
ravine until it dried up.
God helped Elijah to
stay alive and well.

109

Elijah and the widow

1 Kings 17:8–16

When the water in the brook ran dry,
God told Elijah to go to Zarephath, where
a widow would help him.

The widow had very little food. She lived
with her young son. Both were very hungry.
But she offered Elijah all she had left —
a handful of flour in a jar and a little oil.

Elijah told the widow to go and make
a small loaf of bread.

"Make some bread for me first, then
for yourselves. God has told me that the
jar of flour will never be empty and
the jug of oil will never run dry, until

the day the rains come again!" said Elijah.
This is exactly what happened. So the
Lord provided again for all Elijah's needs.

Elijah and the prophets of Baal

1 Kings 18:20–24

After three years, God told Elijah to return to King Ahab.

Elijah *spoke boldly* to Ahab: "You have turned away from God and worshiped other gods like Baal instead."

Elijah knew that only his God, the
God of Israel, was real and able to
answer prayer.

"We will have a contest on
Mount Carmel to see who is the
true God," he said. "Get two
bulls. The prophets of Baal can
have one and put it on their altar.
I will put the other on the altar of
the Lord. Then the prophets of
Baal can call upon him to send
fire to burn up their offering.
I will call on God to do the
same. Whoever answers with
fire is the true God."

The contest

1 Kings 18:25–39

The prophets of Baal called to Baal from morning till noon, but there was no fire.

"Shout louder!" said Elijah. "Perhaps Baal is asleep!"

Then Elijah prepared the altar of the Lord. He put the *bull* on it and *soaked* the altar with water. How could it possibly burn now?

Elijah prayed: "Oh, Lord God,

please show these people that You are
the real God. Help them to know
You and worship You again."
Suddenly God sent fire to
burn up the bull on the altar
and all the water around it.
Everyone was amazed!
They threw themselves
to the ground, shouting,
"The Lord is God!"
God had sent fire
and shown King Ahab
that He was the
true God.

Elijah hears God speak

1 Kings 19:10–13

King Ahab's wife was furious with Elijah. He ran away again and hid in a cave.

As he hid in the cave, Elijah heard God's voice saying, "What are you doing, Elijah?"

Elijah answered, "I am the only one left who worships You. They are trying to kill me now too."

God said, "Go and stand on the mountain, for the Lord is soon going to pass by."

A mighty wind blew against the mountain so hard that rocks shattered. But God was not in the wind.

There was a mighty earthquake. But God was not in the earthquake.

There was a great fire. But God was not in the fire.

Then there was a gentle whisper. When Elijah heard it, he hid his face in his cloak and stood at the mouth of the cave. God was in the gentle whisper. He assured Elijah that he was not alone, but that other believers still worshiped God too.

Elijah goes to heaven

1 Kings 19:19–21; 2 Kings 2:11–12

Elijah chose Elisha to be the next prophet. Elisha became his close friend and helper.

At the end of Elijah's life, Elijah and Elisha were travelling along a road from Gilgal.

"I will not leave you," said Elisha to Elijah.

Suddenly a chariot of fire and horses of fire appeared. Then Elijah went up to heaven in a whirlwind.

Elisha watched and cried out, "My father! My father! The chariots and horsemen of Israel!" Elijah was gone from his sight.

Elisha heals Naaman

2 Kings 5

Naaman was an army general in another country.

Naaman had a skin disease called leprosy, which made his skin turn very white and sore. None of the doctors could help him.

He and his wife looked after a little girl from Israel. The little girl told Naaman about Elisha.

"God uses him to make people well again!" she said to Naaman.

So Naaman *set out* to *see* Elisha.
But Elisha would not *see* Naaman.

He just sent a rather strange message:
"Wash seven times in the River Jordan.
You will be healed."

Naaman wasn't sure he wanted to do
that, but eventually he did as
Elisha told him. He washed
seven times in the river...
and his skin was made
completely better!

Naaman thanked
Elisha and praised God
for healing him.

Daniel in a strange land

Daniel 1

King Nebuchadnezzar of Babylon captured the King of Judah and stole treasures from the great Temple in Jerusalem. He also commanded that some of Israel's most handsome young men be brought back to Babylon. He brought Daniel and three friends, whom the king named Shadrach, Meshach, and Abednego. Nebuchadnezzar wanted them to study at the royal court for three years to

learn all about Babylon and study great books. Then they would serve the King.

The king wanted to give the young men food and drink, but they refused it because the King had offered it first to other gods. Instead they ate only vegetables and drank water.

Daniel and his friends were a long way from home. But they prayed to God and worked hard. They soon became the wisest and cleverest men in Babylon.

The king's dream

Daniel 2:1–47

King Nebuchadnezzar had a terrible nightmare. None of his wise men could explain the meaning of his dream. The king was very angry. He warned the wise men that he would kill them all if they couldn't help.

So Daniel asked God to show him the dream and its meaning.

The next day, he went to the king and explained what God had shown him. The king had seen a huge statue with a golden head, chest and arms of silver, a bronze body, iron legs, and clay feet. A stone from a mountain hit the feet, which crumbled, and the whole statue came crashing down.

124

"Your majesty," said Daniel. "You are indeed a great ruler, but after you will come three more kingdoms. Then God will set up a kingdom that will never fall."

The king bowed down low.

"Now I believe that your God is above all other gods," he said.

The fiery furnace

Daniel 3

King Nebuchadnezzar ordered everyone to bow down to his huge, golden statue. But Daniel's friends—Shadrach, Meshach, and Abednego—refused because this went against God's command.

"Then throw them into the fiery furnace!" said the king angrily.

"God will save us," said Shadrach, Meshach, and Abednego.

The king ordered his men to heat the furnace seven times hotter than usual. Soldiers tied up Shadrach, Meshach, and Abednego and threw them in.

The king watched.

Then, "Look!" he shouted. "There are four men in the furnace! They are all walking around, completely unharmed! The fourth man looks like a god!"

The king ordered his soldiers to let the men out. They were not burned at all. God really had saved them!

Then Nebuchadnezzar believed in the one true God too.

Thrown to the lions!

Daniel 6:6–28

King Darius was very upset. He had been tricked into making a new law that everyone had to pray to him. But Daniel prayed only to God. King Darius liked Daniel. But he had to keep his new law and that meant Daniel was thrown into a den of lions.

"May your God save you!" he shouted to Daniel. A very heavy stone was rolled over the door of the den. The King could not sleep that night for worry.

Early the next day, he went to the lions' den and shouted to Daniel, "Are you alive?"

"Yes! I am alive and well, your Majesty!" replied Daniel. "God sent an angel to close the lions' mouths."

King Darius was overjoyed and commanded everyone to worship God.

Jonah runs away from God

Jonah 1:1–15

"Go to Nineveh!" said God to Jonah.

God was angry with the people of Nineveh because they had forgotten Him.

But Jonah did not want to go to Nineveh. He went aboard a ship and set sail for a distant shore in the opposite direction. He was running away from God.

But Jonah couldn't hide from God.

God sent a mighty storm. The sailors on board the ship thought they would all drown.

"It's my fault!" said Jonah. "I ran away from God! You must throw me into the sea!"

At first the sailors didn't want to throw
Jonah overboard. But the storm became
worse and they were in great danger.
So they threw Jonah out of the boat.

As soon as Jonah sank down into the
dark water, the storm stopped.

131

Jonah and the big fish

Jonah 1:17; 2:10–3:5

But God saved Jonah from drowning.

He sent an enormous fish to come and swallow up Jonah. Inside the fish, Jonah prayed to God.

"Thank You for saving me!" he prayed. "You are a great God."

Jonah stayed inside the fish for three days and three nights. It was very dark and smelly. Then the fish spat him out onto a beach.

"Now go to Nineveh!" said God.

This time Jonah did as God said.

Jonah told the people of Nineveh that God wanted to show His love for them. He gave them a chance to say they were sorry for all the wrong things they had done and He forgave them.

The New Testament

Mary meets an angel

Luke 1:26–38, 46–55

God sent the angel Gabriel to a little town called Nazareth. He had come to give wonderful news to a virgin named Mary.

"Mary!" said Gabriel. "Don't be afraid! God has chosen you. You will have a baby boy and you must call Him Jesus. He will be very great. He will be the Son of God. His kingdom will never end!"

Mary was astonished and afraid, but she said to the angel, "I am God's servant. May it happen as you have said."

Mary sang songs of praise to God for choosing her to be the mother of God.

The journey to Bethlehem

Luke 2:1–5

Mary was soon going to be married to Joseph, a carpenter in Nazareth. Joseph's family came from the town of Bethlehem, many miles away.

Shortly before Mary's baby was due
to be born, Joseph had to return to
Bethlehem to be counted by the Roman
governor. Mary had to go too.

It was a very long, tiring journey.
Joseph walked in front, with Mary a little
way behind. Their donkey carried their
small bundles of clothes, and a water
bottle.

Mary was getting very tired. Her baby
was due to be born quite soon.

When would they reach Bethlehem?

No room at the inn

Luke 2:6–7

At last Mary and Joseph could see the rooftops of Bethlehem in the distance.

They were so tired after their long journey.

But when they arrived in Bethlehem, there was nowhere to stay!

Mary was very worried because her baby was soon to be born. Joseph knocked on many doors in the town, trying to find a room for them to sleep in that night.

140

At last an innkeeper said
they could stay at the back
of his house where the animals slept.
There was no bed, but at
least it was warm and
dry in the straw.

Jesus is born

Luke 2:6–7

The time came for Mary to have her *baby*. She gave birth to a *son*.

Mary called Him Jesus, just as the angel Gabriel had told her to.

Mary wrapped the *baby* warmly in *strips* of cloth and laid Him in the *soft* hay in a manger.

The animals munched their food and shuffled in the straw. Mary gazed down at her little son. He looked so tiny and helpless. Yet the angel Gabriel had said that He was God, come to earth as a baby.

Angels visit the shepherds
Luke 2:8–14

On a hillside near Bethlehem some shepherds were looking after their sheep. Suddenly there was a blinding flash in the sky. It was an angel!

"Don't be afraid!" the angel said. "I have come to bring you good news. This very night a baby has been born

144

in Bethlehem. He is
Christ the Lord!

"You will find the baby
wrapped in strips of cloth and
lying in a manger. Go now and see Him!"

The shepherds could not speak—they
were very frightened and amazed at the
same time. The Savior of the world had
finally come!

Then lots of angels appeared in the sky,
singing, "Glory to God in the highest, and
on earth peace to men!"

The shepherds visit Jesus

Luke 2:15–20

"Hurry!" shouted the shepherds. "We must go to Bethlehem at once to find the baby God has told us about!"

They ran through the town, looking for a newborn baby.

"Is there a baby here?" they asked an innkeeper.

He showed the shepherds through to the back of the house, where the animals slept. There they found Mary and Joseph. And there, in a manger, wrapped in cloths, was the newborn baby: Jesus, their Savior.

The shepherds looked at the tiny baby and felt great joy in their hearts.

They went back to their sheep, praising God for all they had seen. It was just as the angel had said.

147

Wise Men see a new star

Matthew 2:1–2

When Jesus was born in Bethlehem, Wise Men in lands far away in the east spotted a very bright star in the sky. They knew it was a sign.

"A new king is born!" said one Wise Man.

"Let's go and find Him!" said another.

They chose special gifts to take with them, set off, and followed the star.

They traveled over desert, hills, and valleys to find the new King.

Following the star   Matthew 2:1–8

The Wise Men went to the palace of King Herod.

"Do you know where the new King has been born?" they asked Herod.

King Herod was jealous. He wanted to be the only King.

He asked the chief priests and teachers to find out what the Wise Men were talking about.

"It is written in the Scriptures," said one teacher, "that a King will be born in Bethlehem!"

Herod started to make plans.

"Go and find the baby in Bethlehem!" he told the Wise Men. "But please come back and tell me where He is so I can worship Him too."

Jesus at the Temple

Luke 2:22–32

When Jesus was just over a month old, Mary and Joseph took Him to the Temple in Jerusalem. They wanted to say thank You to God.

They took two doves to offer at the Temple.

In the Temple there was a very old man named Simeon who had been waiting all his life to see the Savior. Simeon saw Mary and knew at once that her baby was the special Child

152

he had been
waiting to see.

He took Jesus
in his arms and
thanked God:

"Lord God,
now I may go
in peace, for
I have seen the
Savior, the one who
will bring light to
all the people
of God."

Gifts for the baby King

Matthew 2:9–15

The Wise Men followed the star all the way to Bethlehem, where they found Jesus with His mother, Mary. They were overjoyed to see Him. They bowed down low and worshiped Jesus. Then out of their saddlebags they pulled their fine gifts and gave them to Jesus: gold, frankincense, and myrrh.

God warned
the Wise Men in
a dream not to go
back to King Herod,
so they went home
by a different
road. And God
warned Joseph
to take Mary and
Jesus to Egypt,
where they
would be safe
from wicked
King Herod.

155

Jesus goes missing

Luke 2:41–49

When Jesus was twelve years old, He went to the city of Jerusalem for the Passover feast.

When it was time to go home, Mary and Joseph couldn't see Jesus, but they thought

He was traveling with others. Then Mary began to get very worried and turned back to Jerusalem to look for Jesus.

Three days later, Mary and Joseph found Him. He was in the Temple courts, speaking to the teachers. Everyone was amazed. Jesus knew so much about God!

"My son!" said Mary. "We've been so worried!"

"Mother," said Jesus. "Didn't you know I would be here in My Father's house?"

Jesus is baptized

Luke 3:2–3, 21–22

John the Baptist talked to people about God. He told them to say sorry for the wrong things they had done. Then John baptized them in the water of the River Jordan for the forgiveness of their sins.

When Jesus was about thirty years old, He came to see John on the bank of the river.

"I want you to baptize Me in the river," said Jesus.

John was very surprised. Jesus had done nothing wrong and John thought He didn't need

to be baptized. But he did as Jesus asked.

When Jesus came out of the river, the Holy Spirit came upon Him in the form of a dove, and a voice from heaven spoke: "This is My Son, with whom I am pleased."

It was God's voice.

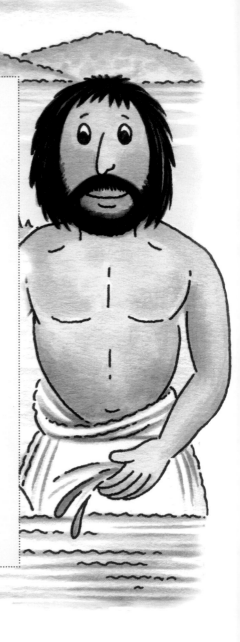

Jesus in the wilderness

Matthew 4

After Jesus was baptized, He went into the wilderness and ate nothing for forty days and nights. When He was very hungry, the devil came and tempted Him.

First, the devil tried to persuade Jesus to turn stones into bread to eat.

Next, Jesus was taken to the top of the Temple and told

to throw Himself off so the angels would catch Him. Last, the devil offered to give Jesus all the kingdoms of the earth if He would only bow down and worship him. But Jesus did not give in to any of the devil's tricks.

"Away from Me!" Jesus said.

He spoke words from the Scriptures to the devil until he went away and left Jesus alone. Then angels came to be with Jesus.

The wedding at Cana

John 2:1–10

Jesus was a guest at a wedding in Cana. There was a great feast and everyone was really enjoying the celebration. Suddenly the wine began to run out.

"You must do something," said Mary, Jesus' mother.

But Jesus already knew what God wanted Him to do.

He told the servants to fill six large stone jars with water, then take them to the man in charge of the feast. When the man tasted it, he was very pleased.

"That's strange!" said the man. "People usually serve the best wine first, but you have left the best wine till last!"

Jesus had actually turned water into wine!

Jesus calls the disciples

Luke 5:1–11

One day Jesus was speaking to large crowds of people on the shore of Lake Galilee. He was telling them about God's kingdom.

Jesus saw two fishermen's boats on the shore. He stepped into a boat belonging to Simon and spoke to the crowds from the boat.

When He had finished speaking, Jesus asked Simon to row the boat out into the deeper water and let down the nets.

"We've worked hard all night," said Simon, "and haven't caught a single fish. But if You tell me, I'll do it."

So off they went. They let down their nets and when they pulled them

back up, they were filled to overflowing with fish!

Simon couldn't believe his eyes. Neither could James and John, Simon's partners.

"Don't be afraid," said Jesus. "Follow Me. I will make you fishers of men."

The fishermen left their nets and followed Jesus.

Jesus makes a man walk again

Luke 5:17–26

Jesus was inside a house, talking to the teachers of the Law. Suddenly, they heard a rustling noise above them and saw a large hole appear in the ceiling!

Faces peered through the hole, and a man on a mat was lowered down through the hole. The man could not walk and he wanted to see Jesus very badly. His friends could not bring him through the door because of the huge crowds, so they had taken him to the roof and thought of another way in— through the ceiling!

Jesus looked at the man kindly.

"Your sins are forgiven," He said. "Stand up! Pick up your mat and walk."

At once the man stood up and walked home on his strong legs, thanking God for what Jesus had done.

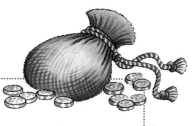

Jesus and the tax collector

Luke 5:27–32

Matthew was a tax collector. Everyone hated tax collectors, so Matthew was often unhappy and alone.

Jesus stopped to talk to Matthew as he was sitting at his usual place to collect the taxes.

"Come and follow Me!" He said kindly.

Matthew stood up and went away with Jesus.

Matthew held a big feast that day for Jesus at his home. He invited other tax collectors and friends.

Some teachers of the Law complained.
"Why do You eat and drink with those
people?" they asked.

Jesus heard what they were saying and
answered, "It is not healthy people who
need a doctor,
but those who
are ill. Go and
think about what
that means."

Jesus wanted
everyone to know
that they could
come to God
and be forgiven.

169

The wise and foolish builders

Luke 6:46–49

Jesus once told this story:

"Anyone who listens to My words and does what I say is like a wise man who built his house upon a rock," said Jesus.

"The rain poured down, the wind blew hard, the rivers rose and tried to wash the house away. But the man had built his house on a strong foundation. It didn't budge.

"But if you don't listen to what I say, you are like a foolish man who built his house upon the sand.

"The rain poured down, the wind blew

hard, the rivers rose and tried to wash the house away. And the house fell down with an enormous CRASH!"

The soldier's servant

Matthew 8:5–13

Crowds followed Jesus everywhere, watching to see what He would do for people who were sick or blind. He did amazing things!

One day, a Roman officer came to Jesus for help.

"My servant is very ill," he said. "He is too ill to leave the house."

Jesus replied, "Then I will go to your house and make him well."

"No, no," said the officer.

"I know how busy You are. But if You just say the word, I know he will be healed."

Jesus was very pleased to find that the officer had great faith in Him.

"Go home, then," said Jesus. "What you believe will be done."

The officer ran home. He found to his great joy that his servant had been made well again!

The sower

Luke 8:4–15

Jesus told this story to a large crowd on the shores of Lake Galilee:

"A man went to sow some corn. Some seed fell along the path where birds came and ate it. Some seed fell on rocky ground where the corn could not grow.

"Some seed fell among thorn bushes that choked the plants.

"But some of the seeds fell in good soil. The plants grew and produced fine corn and there was a good harvest."

Jesus explained what the story meant:

God is the sower. The seed is His message. Some people hear God's message but forget about Him. Some people try to follow God but give up when trouble comes their way.

Some people become too busy with worries, money, and all kinds of other things.

But other people are like good soil where the seeds can grow and blossom; they hear God's message, follow God, and live for Him.

The hidden treasure

Matthew 13:44

Jesus told another story about what the kingdom of God is like:

"A man found some treasure hidden in a field. It was so beautiful! It sparkled in the sunlight and the man wanted to keep it.

"So the man went away and sold everything that he had in the world, even his clothes! With the money he got, he bought the field with the treasure in it. Now the treasure belonged to him! He was really happy!"

177

Jesus calms the storm

Mark 4:35–41

One day, Jesus and His disciples got into a boat on the lake. It had been a very busy day and Jesus was tired.

Suddenly a fierce storm blew up. The boat bobbed about like a cork and huge waves splashed over the side. The disciples were terrified of sinking! But Jesus was fast asleep.

"Save us, Lord!" they shouted to Jesus.

"Why are you so afraid?" asked Jesus, waking up.

Then Jesus got up and ordered the wind and the waves to calm down. The storm vanished. Everyone was amazed.

"Even the winds and the waves obey Him!" they said.

Jesus brings Jairus's daughter back to life

Mark 5:21–42

One day, hundreds of people were crowding around Jesus.

"Please help me!" begged a man called Jairus. "My daughter is very ill."

As Jesus tried to make His way to Jairus's house, people kept stopping Him.

Then someone from Jairus's house came to Jesus.

"It's too late now," he said. "Jairus's daughter has died!"

"Don't worry," said Jesus to Jairus. "Just believe, and she will be well."

Jesus went to the house with Jairus and three of Jesus' disciples. Everyone was crying loudly and sobbing.

But Jesus said, "Don't worry! She is not dead. She is only asleep."

He took the girl by the hand and said, "Get up!"

She came back to life and sat up.

"Give her something to eat," said Jesus.

Jairus and the girl's mother were overjoyed to see their daughter alive again.

Jesus feeds five thousand people

John 6:1–13

Jesus was speaking to a large crowd of men, women, and children. They had been listening to Him all day and were getting hungry.

Jesus wanted to feed them.

"Where can we buy food for all these people?" He asked His disciples.

Philip replied, "We would need more than two hundred silver coins to buy enough!"

Andrew said, "There is a boy here who says he will share his lunch. But he has only five loaves and two small fishes."

Jesus took the food, thanked God, then shared it with everyone!

No one went away hungry. Jesus gave them all enough to eat, and there were even twelve baskets full of leftovers!

The good Samaritan

Luke 10:25–37

A man once asked Jesus, "Who is my neighbor?"
Jesus told the man this story:

"One day, a man was attacked and left for
dead while travelling from Jerusalem to Jericho.

"After some time, a priest travelling that
way saw the injured man lying by the roadside.
But he walked on by.

"Next a temple-worker walked past. He
didn't stop either!

"Finally a man from Samaria came along the
road. He bandaged the wounds of the injured
man, helped him onto his donkey, and took him
to an inn, paying the innkeeper to look after
him until he was better."

Jesus asked, "Who was the poor man's real neighbor?"

"The one who helped him," replied the man.

The man with the barns

Luke 12:16–21

Jesus told this story:

"There was once a young man who was very rich. He stored his crops in a barn. When the barn became too full, he thought he would just build bigger barns. Then he said to himself, "Now I've stored up good things for many years. I'll eat, drink, and take life easy.

"But God spoke to him: 'You fool! Tonight your life will be taken from you. Who will get all your riches then?'"

Jesus said, "This is how it will be for people who are greedy and keep things for themselves but do not give much to God."

Jesus walks on the water

Matthew 14:22–33

Jesus' disciples set off in a boat to cross the lake and go to Capernaum. A stormy wind blew and waves rocked the boat. The men kept on rowing, but they were scared.

Suddenly they saw someone coming toward them. He was walking on the water! They couldn't believe what they saw and were very afraid.

"Don't be frightened," said Jesus. "You all know Me—your Lord, Jesus."

Only Jesus could walk on water!

They wanted Him to come aboard. At once the boat reached the shore and they were all safe.

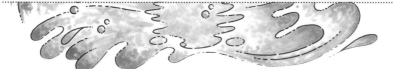

The lost sheep

Luke 15:1–7

Jesus once told a story about a shepherd:

"A shepherd had a hundred sheep. He looked after them all and protected them from wild animals.

"One day the shepherd found that one was missing. So he set out to find his lost sheep, leaving the ninety-nine other sheep in the sheepfold.

"He looked high and low, behind bushes and rocks. Where could the sheep be?

"Suddenly the shepherd heard faint bleating: he had found his lost sheep!

"He picked it up lovingly and carried it home on his shoulders.

"He was so pleased to have found his lost sheep that he invited all his neighbors to a party.

"God is like that shepherd," said Jesus. "He cares even if only one of His sheep is lost."

The prodigal son

Luke 15:11–24

Jesus once told a story about a son who left home
with his share of his inheritance:

"The father loved his son and was very sad.

"The son did many things and spent all the
money very quickly. But then nobody wanted to be
his friend anymore. He had to find a job feeding
pigs and he was hungry.

"'I must go to Dad and ask to work on the
farm,' he thought.

"As he came near to his home, he saw his
father running toward him. The son he loved had
come back. How happy that made him!

"That father was like God," Jesus explained.
"He waits to forgive anyone who comes back
to Him to say they are sorry."

The rich young man

Luke 18:18–30

A rich young ruler asked Jesus, "What must I do to live with God forever?"

"Do what God tells you in the Ten Commandments," said Jesus.

"I've kept them all my life," said the young man.

194

"Then sell everything you have and give it all to the poor," said Jesus. "Come, follow Me."

The young man was very sad because he was very rich and didn't want to give away all his wealth.

Jesus said, "It is hard for rich people to enter God's kingdom. It is easier for a camel to go through the eye of a needle!"

The man with leprosy

Matthew 8:1–4

Jesus went with His disciples to a nearby town. They met a man there who had a terrible skin disease called leprosy. His skin had turned all white. Nobody went near the man. He was very lonely.

When the man saw Jesus coming, he threw himself at Jesus' feet, crying, "Lord, You can make me well again, if You want to."

Jesus put His hand on the man and said, "Yes, I do want to make you well. Be well again!" All at once, the man's skin turned a normal color and he was

completely well again!

Jesus told him not to tell anyone about it, but to go to the priest:

"Show him that you are well again and offer a gift to God. Everyone will know that God has healed you."

News about Jesus spread throughout the town.

Jesus blesses children

Luke 18:15–17

People loved to bring their children to Jesus for Him to bless them.

Jesus welcomed them with open arms.

But Jesus' disciples thought He had more important things to do than talk to children.

"Don't bother Him with the children," they said to the mothers and fathers.

Jesus overheard them and became angry.

"Let the children come to Me!" He said. "Don't try to stop them!

"My Kingdom belongs to people who are like these children. You will never enter God's kingdom if you don't enter it like a child."

Jesus makes a blind man see

Mark 8:22–25

One day people brought a blind man to Jesus. They wanted Jesus to help him to see again.

Jesus walked out of the village with the man. Then Jesus spat on the man's eyes and gently put His hands on them.

"Can you see anything yet?" asked Jesus.

"I can see some people, but they are all fuzzy, like trees walking around."

So Jesus put His hands on the man's eyes a second time. This time the man opened his eyes and could see perfectly! He was amazed to see the colorful world and the kind face of Jesus.

Zacchaeus

Luke 19:1–10

Jesus was walking through Jericho. A man named Zacchaeus lived there. He was a very rich man and was in charge of collecting taxes in the area.

Zacchaeus was a very short man. He heard that Jesus was coming, but he wasn't tall enough to see over the heads of the crowd. So he climbed a tree to see Jesus.

Jesus called to him in the tree: "Zacchaeus, come down! I want to come to your house today."

Zacchaeus was very pleased to welcome Jesus to his house. But other people started complaining, "Zacchaeus is a bad man! Why does Jesus want to eat with him?"

Zacchaeus later told the crowds of people that he was going to be nicer to everyone.

"I want to give half of all I own to the poor. If I have cheated anyone, I will pay them back four times as much."

The wise and foolish girls

Matthew 25:1–13

Jesus told a story about ten girls at a wedding:

"There were once ten girls who were supposed to meet the bridegroom on his way to the wedding. They carried oil lamps to light the way. But the oil didn't last long in the lamps.

"Five of the girls remembered to bring extra oil with them. But the other

five had forgotten. Their lamps went out and they had to run off to buy more.

"While they were away, the bridegroom arrived. The five girls whose lamps were burning brightly met him and went with him to the wedding. The door was shut.

"When the other five girls finally arrived, they were too late for the wedding!"

Jesus said we should be like the wise girls and be ready for Him when He comes again.

The widow's pennies

Mark 12:41–44

Jesus was in the Temple in Jerusalem, watching people putting money into the collecting box. The money was an offering to God.

Some rich people were giving a lot of money.

Chink! The coins clinked in the box very loudly. Everyone stopped and watched. The rich people felt very pleased with themselves.

Then a very poor widow shuffled toward the collecting box. She didn't want anyone to notice her. She was ashamed that she had only two very small coins to give to God.

Clink! The two small coins dropped softly into the box.

The widow moved quietly away. Jesus told His disciples to come closer to Him.

"Let Me tell you," He said, "that poor widow has just given more than anyone else.

"Everyone else gave what they didn't really need. But this widow gave everything she has to God."

Lazarus

John 11:1–44

Jesus had a good friend named Lazarus, who lived in a town many miles away. Jesus heard that Lazarus was ill. But by the time Jesus reached the town, Lazarus was dead.

Jesus wept. He went to the tomb where Lazarus's body was put. It had been there for four days already. A large stone was rolled across the tomb.

Jesus told some men to roll the stone aside. He prayed aloud to God: "Thank You, Father, that You hear My prayers."

Then Jesus shouted, "Come out, Lazarus!"

Lazarus walked out into the daylight, still covered in his grave clothes and with a cloth over his face, but he was alive again!

Many people watching now knew that Jesus had been sent from God and they put their trust in Him.

A welcome for the King

Matthew 21:1–9

Jesus and His disciples were going to Jerusalem for the Passover festival.

Jesus sent two of His followers ahead, saying, "Go to the village over there and find a young donkey. Bring it to Me. Say that your master needs it."

The two friends fetched the donkey and put their cloaks over the donkey's back.

Jesus rode into the great city of Jerusalem. Huge crowds came to greet Jesus, spreading their cloaks on the road and waving palm branches.

"Hosanna to the Son of David! Blessed is He who comes in the name of the Lord!" they shouted.

They cheered and waved to Jesus, their King.

Jesus in the Temple

Matthew 21:12–13

When Jesus arrived in Jerusalem, He went to the Temple. He wanted to pray to God in the holy place of this noisy, bustling city.

But when Jesus entered the Temple area, He became very angry indeed. There were people buying and selling animals and doves, and other people were changing money. The Temple had become a noisy, smelly marketplace, just like the rest of the city.

Jesus turned over the tables with a great crash. The doves flew away. The people behind the tables were shocked. What was Jesus doing?

"You are turning the Temple into a place for robbers!" shouted Jesus. "It is written, 'My house shall be called a house of prayer!'"

Jesus wanted to keep the Temple a holy place. But what He did made many people angry. The chief priests and teachers of the Law began to make plans to get rid of Jesus.

213

Mary's gift to Jesus

Mark 14:3–9

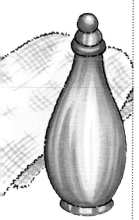

Shortly before the Passover festival, Jesus went to eat at a friend's house. A woman named Mary came up to Jesus holding a very precious jar. It was made of alabaster and inside was something very special.

Mary opened the jar. The smell of perfume came out. Mary had brought some very expensive perfume for Jesus. She poured it over His head.

"What's she doing?" asked some of Jesus' disciples. "That's a real waste of money, just pouring it away like that!"

Jesus heard them complaining and said, "Leave her alone. She has done a beautiful thing for Me to prepare My body for burial."

215

Judas betrays Jesus

Matthew 26:14–16

The chief priests wanted to get rid of Jesus. But they didn't know how to capture Him.

Judas Iscariot, one of Jesus' disciples, was very greedy for money. He thought of a plan to get rich quickly.

Judas went to the chief priests and asked, "What will you pay me if I hand Jesus over to you?"

"We'll give you thirty pieces of silver," they said.

216

"I'll do it!" said Judas.
Judas watched
for a chance to
hand Jesus
over to them.
He was no
longer a friend
of Jesus. Judas
was His enemy.

Jesus washes His disciples' feet John 13:4-14

Jesus knew He would not be with His disciples for much longer. He wanted to celebrate the Passover meal with them one last time.

Jesus met His twelve disciples at the upper room of a house in Jerusalem.

Jesus took a bowl of water and began to wash His disciples' feet.

"You mustn't wash my feet!" said Peter. "You are our Master, not our servant!"

"Unless I do, you don't belong to Me," said Jesus.

"Then wash my hands
and head as well!"
said Peter.
    Jesus washed
Peter's feet.
    "Now that
I have washed
your feet," said
Jesus, "you must
also wash each
other's feet.
Do as I have done."

219

The Last Supper Matthew 26:19–30

After Jesus had finished washing everyone's feet, He lay at the table with His disciples, ready to eat the Passover meal. The meal was lamb, bread without yeast, bitter herbs, and wine. It was a special time of remembering how God had rescued Moses and the Israelites in Egypt many years ago.

Jesus looked at His disciples gathered round Him and said, "One of you is going to hand Me over to be killed."

His friends were very worried.

"Surely not I!" they all said.

Jesus already knew it would be Judas Iscariot.

While they were eating, Jesus took the
bread, broke it, and gave it to His disciples.
"Eat this and remember Me,"
said Jesus.

222

"This is My body."

Then He took the cup of wine, thanked God for it, and handed it round.

"Drink this and remember Me," said Jesus. "This is My blood, given for you for the forgiveness of sins."

Jesus' disciples drank the wine. They sang a song together, then went away to the Mount of Olives.

223

Gethsemane

Matthew 26:36–41

On the Mount of Olives was a garden called
Gethsemane. Here Jesus knelt down to pray
to God. He knew that the time was coming
for Him to be taken away. He was very sad.
Tears ran down His face as He prayed to
God, His Father.

Jesus asked His disciples to pray with
Him. But they kept falling asleep.

"Why are you sleeping?" He asked them.
"Watch and pray with Me."

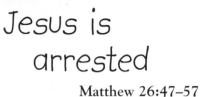

Jesus is arrested

Matthew 26:47–57

Suddenly a crowd came toward them and Judas Iscariot was with them. Soldiers and chief priests followed closely behind. Judas came near to Jesus to kiss Him. This showed the soldiers where Jesus was.

One of Jesus' disciples took out a sword and chopped off the ear of

the high priest's servant!

"Put that sword away!" said Jesus. "All who use the sword will die by the sword. Things must happen in this way."

Jesus touched the servant's ear and healed it.

Jesus was arrested and taken away to see the high priest.

Peter pretends
he doesn't know Jesus

Matthew 26:69–75

Jesus' other disciples were very upset, especially Peter. Earlier that evening, Jesus had warned Peter:

"Before the rooster crows tonight, you will say three times that you do not know Me."

Peter couldn't understand it. Jesus was his friend! Peter wouldn't let Him down.

But while Peter was waiting to see what would happen to Jesus, some girls came up to him and asked if he was a friend of Jesus.

"No," said Peter. "I don't know what you are talking about!"

They asked him three times and each time he said, "No!"

Then suddenly a rooster crowed. Peter remembered what Jesus had said.

Peter felt terrible and cried. He had wanted to be faithful to Jesus, but now he really had let Jesus down.

Jesus is taken to Pilate

Mark 15:1–20

The soldiers who were guarding Jesus were very cruel to Him. Then Jesus was brought before Pilate, the Roman governor. "What has this man done wrong?" Pilate asked the crowd.

"He is causing trouble all over the country," said the chief priests. "He says He is a King."

"Are you the king of the Jews?" asked Pilate.

"Yes, it is as you say," said Jesus.

"What shall I do with Jesus?" Pilate asked the crowd.

"Crucify Him!" the people shouted.

Pilate did not think Jesus had done anything wrong, but he wanted to please the crowd. So he handed Jesus over to the soldiers to be killed. The soldiers put a purple robe on Jesus and a crown of thorns on His head.

Jesus dies on a cross

Mark 15:22–37

Jesus was taken by the soldiers to a place called Golgotha. There He was nailed to a cross. Above His head was a sign,

"The King of the Jews."
Jesus' mother, Mary,
stood close by and
watched. How could
they do this to her
precious son?

Darkness covered
the land. At the ninth
hour, Jesus cried out in
a loud voice to God, then
breathed His last breath.
Jesus died.

A Roman soldier near
the cross saw this. He
said, "Truly, this man was
the Son of God."

234

The women find the tomb empty

Luke 24:1–3

Early on Sunday morning, the third day after Jesus died, some of the women went to His tomb with special spices.

But what a shock they had when they got there! The large stone that blocked the entrance to the tomb had been rolled away! When they looked inside, they did not see Jesus' body.

The tomb was empty!

"Jesus is alive!"

Luke 24:4–8

Jesus' body was gone. All that was left were the strips of cloth Jesus' body had been wrapped in.

Suddenly two men in bright shining clothes appeared.

"Don't look for Jesus here," they said. "He is alive! Remember that He told you He would die and rise again on the third day."

The women
suddenly remembered.
They ran home
at once and told
Jesus' apostles.
Very soon they
all saw Jesus
again for them-
selves. It was
true! Jesus really
was alive!

The amazing catch of fish

John 21:1–6

Over the next few days, Jesus appeared to His disciples and many others and showed them He really was alive again.

Peter and a group of disciples were out fishing in their boat. Early the next morning, Jesus came to see them and stood on the shore. He was far away, so they did not recognize Him.

"Haven't you caught any fish?" He shouted to the fishermen.

"No!" said Peter.

238

"Then throw your net on the other side of the boat," said Jesus, "and you will catch plenty!"

The men did as He said and sure enough, their nets were filled to the bursting point with fresh, wriggling fish.

Breakfast on the beach

John 21:7–14

"It's Jesus!" said Peter.

Peter and the other apostles knew that only God could do something so amazing. They knew Jesus was the Lord.

Jesus had made a small fire on the shore to cook some of the fish. He had some bread for them too. His disciples came and sat with Him and ate breakfast on the beach. It was wonderful to be with the Lord Jesus again!

Jesus returns to heaven Acts 1:4–11

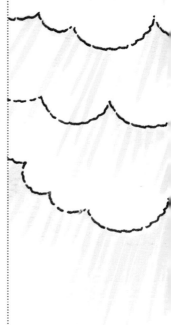

Jesus saw His apostles many times over the next few days and preached about the kingdom of God.

"Don't leave Jerusalem," He told His apostles, "but wait for the gift God has promised—to baptize you with the Holy Spirit. When He comes, you will be able to tell the whole world about Me!"

After forty days, Jesus was taken up to heaven. He was hidden from sight by a cloud.

As the disciples were looking at the sky, two men in white clothes stood beside them.

"Why are you looking at the sky?" they asked the disciples. "Jesus will return one day in the same way as you saw Him go."

The Holy Spirit comes to the believers

Acts 2:1–6

A few days later, on the day of Pentecost, all of Jesus' apostles met together in one place.

Suddenly there was a noise from heaven that sounded like a strong wind blowing. The noise filled the whole house. Then tongues that looked like fire appeared on each one. Everyone was filled with the Holy Spirit and could suddenly speak all kinds of different languages!

There were people in Jerusalem from many different countries, but they could all understand Jesus' apostles speak of the mighty works of God in their own language.

Peter speaks about Jesus

Acts 2:22–42

Peter stood up and told the crowds about Jesus—how He had come to show God's power and be put to death on a cross to pay for their sins. Peter told how God had made

Jesus come alive again to defeat death. And he explained that Jesus kept the promises of the Old Testament.

"Repent and be baptized in the name of Christ for the forgiveness of sin, and you will be given the Holy Spirit," said Peter.

That day, three thousand people were baptized into the Kingdom of God! Jesus' disciples were often in danger. But God helped them not to be afraid. They wanted people all over the world to know the good news that God loves the world so much that He sent His Son, Jesus, to save His people from their sins by dying on the cross.

Where to find the stories in the Bible

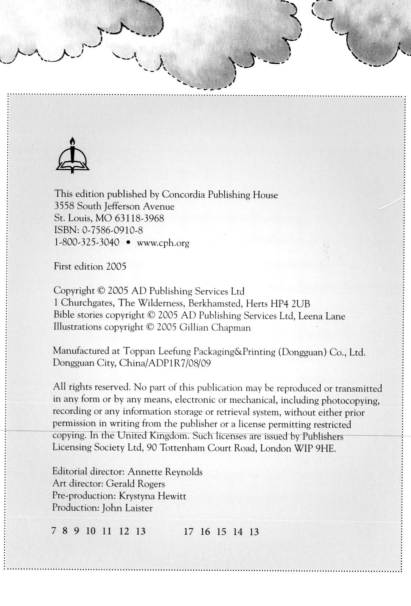

This edition published by Concordia Publishing House
3558 South Jefferson Avenue
St. Louis, MO 63118-3968
ISBN: 0-7586-0910-8
1-800-325-3040 • www.cph.org

First edition 2005

Copyright © 2005 AD Publishing Services Ltd
1 Churchgates, The Wilderness, Berkhamsted, Herts HP4 2UB
Bible stories copyright © 2005 AD Publishing Services Ltd, Leena Lane
Illustrations copyright © 2005 Gillian Chapman

Manufactured at Toppan Leefung Packaging&Printing (Dongguan) Co., Ltd.
Dongguan City, China/ADP1R7/08/09

Editorial director: Annette Reynolds
Art director: Gerald Rogers
Pre-production: Krystyna Hewitt
Production: John Laister

7 8 9 10 11 12 13   17 16 15 14 13